BHEDA

---◄◊►---

Pangnia Budha was the priest of Firozpur's Kalisundari Gudi.... His face was uneven and pockmarked. On the top of his left eyebrow was a tumour as big as a tendu. He was addicted to hemp. His eyes were as red as the raktarani flower.... His greying tangled hair fell to his shoulders, and in it were three plaits with an oleander flower tucked into the longest one. On his shoulder, always, was an axe smeared with vermilion and oil.

Everyone, young or old, was afraid of Pangnia Budha. Children were afraid of his appearance and elders of his sorcery....

Once, it was said, he had practised his black magic on Palsapada's Dama Jhankar.... The moment Dama touched his food the rice turned to leeches and the gruel became blood. To others the plate was merely full of rice. But Dama saw leeches. While the others saw water or rice gruel Dama's eyes saw a bowl of fresh blood. Unable to eat or drink anything ... Dama wasted away and died....

When he saw Laltu, Pangnia Budha stood up saying ... 'I've been waiting for you for a prahara, son. Where have you been?' ...

From his father's smile Laltu understood that there was some hidden purpose behind the old man's visit....

'It seems you have seized Baya's tractor?' asked Dinamastre.

'Why should I seize it? The committee members have seized it.' Laltu's voice was low.

'Who is the committee, son? Isn't it you?' Pangnia Budha emphasized....

'Why do you explain to me, Dadi? As an old man you should understand that without killing the crocodile it is not possible to build a house in water. You better go and tell Baya to do whatever he is capable of doing. Even at the cost of our lives we will not release either the timber or the tractor.'

And then Laltu walked straight into his house. Dinamastre and Pangnia Budha stood speechless.

---◄◊►---

BHEDA

Akhila Naik

Translated from Odia by Raj Kumar

OXFORD
UNIVERSITY PRESS

OXFORD
UNIVERSITY PRESS

Oxford University Press is a department of the University of Oxford.
It furthers the University's objective of excellence in research, scholarship,
and education by publishing worldwide. Oxford is a registered trademark of
Oxford University Press in the UK and in certain other countries.

Published in India by
Oxford University Press
2/11 Ground Floor, Ansari Road, Daryaganj, New Delhi 110 002, India

First published in Odia by Paschima Publications in 2010
This English translation published by Oxford University Press in 2017

ISBN-13: 978-0-19-947607-7
ISBN-10: 0-19-947607-1

Typeset in Trump Mediaeval LT Std 10/16
by Tranistics Data Technologies, New Delhi 110 044
Printed in India by Replika Press Pvt. Ltd

For my daughter Ishita,
a stranger to caste discrimination

Contents

Author's Note

My childhood and youth were spent in a remote village in Odisha's Kalahandi district. My father was a schoolteacher and my mother was an educated housewife. Ours was a lower-middle-class family, which did not have to struggle for food, clothes, books, or stationery. We ate and dressed well and lived in a good house, but the villagers did not treat us well. We were from the Dom community. So the place where we lived was called Dompada. And the place where the so-called upper-caste people lived was called Bhalpada (good *pada*). People of Bhalpada were called *Bhallok* (good people), and those of Dompada, *Domlok*. While the people of Bhalpada, the 'good' people, spoke *Bhalkatha* (good language), the people of Dompada spoke in *Dom* language. In one sense, the meaning of the term Dom was 'bad'. But we were not at all 'bad' people. Why did people hate us, why didn't they touch us, why were there restrictions for us to use the common wells and ponds—I simply could not understand these things till I went to university. I bore all kinds of grief and, as a victim of the caste system, was compelled to live an oppressed life. Only when I went to university did I read the writings of Jotiba Phule, B.R. Ambedkar, Bhima Bhoi, and other non-Brahmin leaders. Going through their writings I began to understand my subjugated self vis-à-vis the Indian caste-bound society.

I started writing at the age of thirteen or fourteen—poems about social and ecological issues of the region where I lived. When I sent some of my poems to the local newspapers for publication they instantly got published. I was very happy to see my poems in print and I remain thankful to the publishers who recognized something worthwhile in my writing and gave me just enough space to express my thoughts. This encouraged me to write more poems, all of which were published regularly in different newspapers and magazines. My first collection of poems came out the same year I wrote my post-graduation examination. With the first collection, there began a discussion among readers on the 'newness' of my poetry. Thereafter, three other anthologies were published. So far as mainstream Odia poetry circle was concerned, I was recognized as a distinct poet. However, I was not at all happy with my poetry because it could not express everything I wanted to say. Was it my inadequacy as a poet or was it the form which was unsuitable for what I wanted to say? It was then that I decided to write a novel. During 1995–6 I began working on a novel in verse. After three to four chapters I simply came to a stop. In 2008, at Ashok Mohanty's request, the editor of the magazine *Pashchima*, I wrote a novel titled *Bheda* which appeared in its October issue. I finished writing it in a fortnight: I cannot say whether or not I was well prepared to write it. I would rather think I was not because when I started writing it, I had no fixed idea about the storyline, sequence of the events, and so on. But the incidents described in the novel had lived in my blood for many years. No incident in the novel is either imaginary or exaggerated; I have witnessed and experienced all of them myself. I know all the characters quite intimately.

Caste-related problems are generally considered to be a social problem. For me they are not just social but also economic and political. In the present-day context we can see how Brahminism, feudalism, and capitalism have united to become a medium of caste exploitation. That is what *Bheda* is about. Again, there are people who consider 'caste' to be an issue of identity politics and nothing more. Such a view is simplistic, narrow, and partial. *Bheda* has made an attempt to show that there are several dimensions to understanding caste. For example, class conflicts within caste communities, gender inequalities, and religious discriminations.

When *Bheda* was published in *Pashchima* in 2008 it created a stir. Many arguments were made regarding the freshness of the content, its treatment, the complexities of ideas and multi-layered events, and the newness of my language and style. It was said that *Bheda* largely used the people's language, which was 'free-flowing' and 'democratic' by nature.

After reading *Bheda*, Professor Raj Kumar from the Department of English, University of Delhi, talked about his interest in translating it into English and, within a short span of time, completed this task. I am grateful to him. I am also equally thankful to Mini Krishnan for proposing its publication.

AKHILA NAIK
4 June 2015

Translator's Note

As a student of literature I must have read hundreds of novels over the years. But after reading *Bheda* I realized that it was the most engaging novel I had ever read. Though not very long, it has a great storyline, an unconventional plot, real characters, complex events, and a new language. All these aspects combine to make *Bheda* a powerful novel. It delves deep into Dalit subjectivity by experimenting with the new social realism. As the first Odia Dalit novel it deals with the theme of caste in contemporary Odia society and exposes its stereotypical caste-mindedness. Such a treatment of caste in Odia literature is rare.

Odia is almost a thousand-year-old language. But barring a few, the majority of the upper-caste Odia litterateurs, who have dominated the Odia literary scene all through the years, have till very recently shied away from addressing questions of caste in the public domain. This does not mean that there are no instances of casteism or caste inequalities in Odisha. As a matter of fact Odia society is casteist to the core and continues to be feudal in many aspects. As a result a modern value system has not been able to enter or influence the many spheres of Odia society to upset the traditional power structure. Thus, Dalits, Adivasis, and other marginalized communities have been pushed to the periphery. Akhila Naik's *Bheda* is the first and only novel in Odia which addresses the discourse of power in the public space. Here, for the first time, the subjects themselves—the Odia Dalits—have their own tales to tell in a realistic mode.

Interestingly the location of these tales is Kalahandi, one of the most backward regions of India of which Naik is a resident. The substance of the stories, characters, and events are real, though presented in fictional form. Since I, too, belong to the same area, I can intimately relate to each character and every situation. Reading the novel I realized that I was reading the stories of my own community. But *Bheda*'s canvas is larger. It comprises the stories of oppressed communities fighting for their freedom.

Reading *Bheda* was no pleasure at all. Being a victim of casteism in a different time and space, while reading it I repeatedly revisited my past and thought about my present. That is when I decided to translate this novel into English and bring the attention of a larger reading public to the relevance of the caste question in contemporary times. But I must confess that translating it from Odia into English was not at all easy. Naik, a student of Odia literature, has used words with precision. More importantly his language is not textbook Odia. He has often used the language of the Kalahandi region spoken by unlettered villagers. To translate those colloquial expressions was a difficult task. I also realized that by translating them into some standard English idioms and phrases they would lose their cultural significance. So I have tried to retain as many spoken words in Odia as possible which, I believe, makes the text richer. The meanings of those words and cultural expressions are provided in a glossary at the end of this book. I hope that the readers will be able to understand the nuances of those terms and acquaint themselves with their cultural significance.

Bheda does not have a linear storyline. Very often the narrative moves back and forth. Therefore, the novelist in some paragraphs has used both the present and the past tense to narrate the sequences of events. When I tried to follow this pattern in English it read awkward. So I have changed the present into the past tense. But however much I tried I could not do justice to the many rhythmic words that Naik has used for specific purposes in the Odia text. Words like *legrelega, bididhungia purohit, bahre mor bamhnen, bahbahre mor marbaden, sakshate ma kalisundri,* and many such local words, which, with strong local specificities, simply failed to come through in the English translation.

Several people helped me in this translation project and I am grateful to each one of them. First of all to Akhila Naik for giving me permission to translate; to Abhishek Das for meticulously going through the first draft; to Debadulal Haldar, Kalyanee Rajan, and Indrani Sen for reading some parts of my translation and commenting on them; to Ashok Mahapatra, Jatindra Kumar Nayak, and Sumanyu Satpathy for offering important suggestions for the Introduction; and to Bhupinder Singh for providing valuable insight while going through the entire manuscript. I sincerely express my gratitude to Mini Krishnan for her meticulous editing. She worked passionately from the beginning to the end and brought perfection to the text. Had it not been for her hard work, patience, and perseverance the book would not have taken its present form.

I am also equally grateful to my family members. While preparing the manuscript I received love and affection from my parents and in-laws. My wife Bedamati continuously helped me in preparing the manuscript. The book is as much her labour of love as it is mine. My daughter Ishita closely followed the translation and often offered suggestions, even though she cannot read Odia. She was so linked to *Bheda* that by now she knows everything about it. By reading the English translation she has been able to familiarize herself with some parts of Odia society, culture, and tradition. This translation, therefore, is as special to her as it is for me. It is for her keen interest on the subject that I offer her the English translation of *Bheda* as a special gift.

RAJ KUMAR
17 March 2017

Introduction

Akhila Naik's *Bheda* has the distinction of being the first Odia Dalit novel. Why did it take so long for an Odia Dalit to write a novel when the first Odia novel, Umesh Chandra Sarkar's *Padmamali*, appeared as early as 1888? The answer lies in the anti-Dalit structure of Odia society and the upper castes' discrimination against the lower castes, including Adivasis. The main theme of *Bheda* is caste violence. In analysing the novel I have closely studied how Dalits in Odisha have been victims of caste atrocities over the years. Odia society has witnessed several social protest movements in different periods of time, and I have tried to trace them to bring a contextual relevance to the Dalit movement and Dalit literature in Odisha. But before we begin to address the caste questions in the novel let us examine how the idea of caste operates in Odia civil society.

Caste and existential situations of Dalits in Odisha

Dalits in Odisha, as elsewhere in India, have been victims of caste oppression for centuries. Predominantly rural and illiterate, they have become one of society's most exploited peripheral groups. Over the years they have lived in subhuman conditions and have suffered economic exploitation, cultural subjugation, and political powerlessness. Even so many years after Independence many civic and other amenities are not available to them; this is because Odisha is a feudal state where many modern and democratic agencies have not been able to upset the traditional power structure. A report prepared by the National Institute of Social Work and Social Sciences, Bhubaneswar, in 1984 highlights the existential conditions of Dalits in Odisha. According to it:

> Out of the surveyed states, Orissa is one where public places were not accessible to the Harijans in almost all the surveyed villages, although [the] violent incidents are not reported in equal measure[s]. The reasons may be the general backwardness and powerlessness as also the low level of awareness of the Scheduled Castes, who continue to bear the social injustices perpetrated on them. (Nayak 1984: 111)

Living in such a hostile environment where insecurity reigns, Odia Dalits always have to work hard and lead a life of compromise, alienation, and resignation. According to the 2011 census Odisha has seventy-five Dalit communities, constituting 18 per cent of the state's population. Following the Hindu caste structure Dalit communities, too, have rigid internal hierarchies among themselves, and inter-caste dining and inter-caste marriages are still not allowed between any two Dalit communities. Dalit politics in the state is fragmented, as Dalits are divided into too many groups and subgroups. They also follow different religious practices. Due to these problems Dalits cannot come together to voice their grievances. They are split and fragmented, each carrying the tag of being a Dalit.

It is sad that today when people are talking about human rights and social justice, Odia Dalits have not been able to unite and raise their voices against inhuman caste practices. Odia society, being feudal in many aspects, does not allow people from the lower castes to exercise many civil and democratic rights enshrined in the Indian Constitution. The Brahmins, Karanas, and Khandayats, and other upper-caste communities still wield what might be called historical power and continue to exploit and oppress the Dalits. As a result the condition of Dalits is miserable. Though they can move freely in towns and cities there are several restrictions on them in villages where they are still confined to the outskirts. For example, they are barred from walking or cycling on certain roads as they are believed to carry their 'pollution' with them. They are not allowed to enter temple premises. Even though they can go to schools, they are not allowed to sit with the upper-caste children. They have separate wells, and in the ponds there are separate ghats for them to take a bath. There are separate burial grounds as well. To this day such discriminations are practised, strengthening the walls and barriers of social difference.

Though education might significantly improve their position, both socially as well as economically, Dalits have never been able to get their benefits on a large scale due to typical structural problems in Odisha. Many sociologists and anthropologists have studied the social structures that exist in Odisha. For example, the American anthropologist James M. Freeman, in his 1978 study of untouchability at a village called Kapileswar (now a part of Bhubaneswar), reveals how the high-caste people deny the lower castes access to educational institutions. Freeman interviewed Muli, an untouchable narrator, who said:

The villagers never forgot, nor did they let us forget that we were untouchables. High-caste children sat inside the school;

the Bauri children about twenty of us, sat outside on the veranda and listened. The two teachers, a Brahmin outsider, and temple servant refused to touch us, even with a stick. To beat us, they threw bamboo canes. The higher caste children threw mud at us. Fearing severe beatings we dared not fight back. (Freeman 1978: 90)

Even today Dalits in Odisha have hardly got equal opportunities for education. As a result the literacy percentage of Dalits remains quite low. This has led to serious problems. Apart from not getting any secure jobs due to illiteracy the Dalits in Odisha cannot avail of many of the constitutional provisions that guarantee them a life of dignity and self-respect. Struggling to meet their daily livelihood Odia Dalits, therefore, cannot think of organizing a movement against their oppressors. That no militant movement or rebellion on the part of Dalits has taken place against their upper-caste Hindu counterparts in the state does not indicate the absence of socio-economic inequalities. It only underlines the fact that Odia Dalits have endured caste oppression silently. One reason for this could be that the socio-economic life of Dalits in Odisha has not undergone the same level of change as that of Dalits elsewhere, for example, in Maharashtra. History testifies that a few cases of unorganized, sporadic resistance did take place but they were swiftly suppressed. It may be necessary to mention here that whenever there has been any protest against caste oppression, the upper castes always succeeded in appropriating the dissenting voices. As a result the voices of the oppressed gradually fade away. This is quite clear when we traverse the pages of Odisha's sociocultural and literary history.

Social protest movements in medieval Odisha

Dalits have endured social inequity, injustice, and indignity through the ages, though not always silently. It is true that violent eruptions of frustration and anger have been rare; however, many voices, particularly in literary forms since the fifteenth century, have been raised against inequality and injustice. Sudramuni Sarala Dasa in the fifteenth century was the pioneer of the social protest movement, which Odisha witnessed during medieval times. Sarala Dasa is known for three major works—*Odia Mahabharata*, *Bilanka Ramayana*, and *Chandi Purana*. These were written in the language of the common people and dealt with topical and mundane events. Thus, he was protesting against the courtly poets and writers (who wrote in Sanskrit), against the language of dominance and power, and about royal characters and elitist themes. Sarala Dasa was a Sudra by caste. At a time when Hindu orthodoxy was at its peak we find that Sarala Dasa managed to articulate the voice of the marginalized, critiquing the Hindu social order; this was no mean achievement for a Sudra.

Sarala Dasa's protest was carried on by five saint-poets who dominated Odia literature for a century, from 1450 to 1550. These poets were Balarama Dasa, Jagannatha Dasa, Achyutanda Dasa, Jasobanta Dasa, and Ananta Dasa, collectively known as the Panchasakhas. Except for Jagannatha Dasa, a Brahmin, the rest of them were Sudras by caste. They rejected the dominance of Sanskrit in literature and espoused the cause of the vernacular as the medium of expression, thus contributing towards the use of everyday Odia in the literature of their region. In fact they followed the path that Sarala Dasa paved as a pioneer and rendered the sacred books of Hindus into the common language in order to make them available to the people. Balaram Dasa's *Jagmohan Ramayan* and *Lakshmi Puran*, Jagannatha Dasa's *Odia Bhagabata*, Achyutananda Dasa's *Harivamsa*, Jasobanta Dasa's *Premabhakti Brahmagita*, and Ananta Dasa's *Hetudaya Bhagabata* are the foremost examples of this development.

These saint-poets also protested against the rigidities of life in temples and monasteries, and sought to rise above the prejudices and debates that had reduced religion to the level of an intellectual polemic. In the process they had to face opposition, criticism, and even conspiracy from the orthodox pundits, who instigated the kings against them. In spite of various repressive measures taken by the establishment the movement could not be curbed fully, even if it had to compromise eventually with the dominant Brahminical system.

After the Panchasakhas the tradition of writing protest literature, which focused on and depicted people's lives and language, came to an abrupt end. A remarkable change in the approach of literature, both in theme as well as in style, is clearly discernible. The lead was taken by the princes such as Dhananjaya Bhanja and Upendra Bhanja of the eighteenth century, who were acquainted with the themes and preoccupations of old Sanskrit works, their forms, and their ornate style and articulations. Their literary works were bound to be aristocratic and there was no hint of reform or revolution in their writing.

Bhima Bhoi and his protest against the Hindu social order

Protest literature was once again retrieved from the religious realm by Bhima Bhoi. Born into a Kondh Adivasi family, Bhoi was the follower of Mahima Dharma, an autochthonous religious movement which made its presence felt in Odisha in the nineteenth century and drafted most of its followers from the oppressed classes of society, the Dalits and the Adivasis. Bhima Bhoi was a poet of distinction who composed several poems and wrote philosophical treatises. His most widely known works are *Stuti Chintamani*, *Srutinisedha Gita*, and *Nirbeda Sadhana*. Apart from these there are scores of 'Mahima' bhajans, whose language is so simple that even an illiterate person can memorize them. Like his predecessors Bhoi attacked orthodox rituals and customs of Odia society. His literary works sought to redefine and redesign societal norms, manners, and behaviour, promising the poor a better world.

Inspired by Bhima Bhoi some of the followers of Mahima dharma organized a protest march in 1874 to burn the idols of Puri Jagannath temple, claiming that Lord Jagannath did not belong to the higher castes but to the original inhabitants of the state, the Adivasis and the Dalits. It may be mentioned here that Jagannath was originally an Adivasi god belonging to the Savara tribe. With the connivance of the Raja–Brahmin nexus the tribal god, in course of time, was Hinduized and Brahminized so much that Adivasis and Dalits are not allowed to enter the temple to this day. Thus, Bhoi's religio-literary consciousness gave birth to an incipient organization and movement venturing into the newly emerging public sphere.

Of course Bhoi's ideas and activities represented a consciousness that targeted the impurities in Hindu society, which did not hesitate to oppress and suppress its own members for no fault of theirs. However, his message could not flower into multiple expressions and movements due to the existential situation of Dalits in Odisha. For a long time, even under colonial rule, Dalits in Odisha could not take advantage of the benefits of elementary education. In fact the British came to Odisha as late as 1803 and, therefore, many of the modern facilities like roads, railways, telephones, and telegraphs were introduced only towards the beginning of the twentieth century. As one of the feudal states in India, Odisha did not go through structural changes that would otherwise have extended several opportunities to the most oppressed groups. It was only after Independence that a sizeable number of Dalits made a belated entry into civil society through literacy and education. However, plans for their education, though announced as government policy, could not spread effectively because of structural inequalities, economic imbalances, and political chicanery. Unlike other places missionary supports for Dalit education came late to Odisha.

The progressives and Odia nationalism

Due to illiteracy and lack of exposure in Odisha, Ambedkar failed to provoke literary articulation among Dalits in Odia. However, during the same period we find some writings on Dalits by upper-caste writers, mainly within the overarching ideology of nationalism. Kalindi Charan Panigrahi, Godabaris Mahapatra, Radha Mohan Gadanayak, Bhagabati Charana Panigrahi, Sachi Routray, Gopinath Mohanty, Kanhu Charan Mohanty, and Basant Kumar Satpathy are some of the upper-caste writers who represented lower-caste characters in their writings. Whether such a representation of Dalits amounts to 'Dalit' literature is a question that needs to be explored, but amongst Dalits there is strong resistance to 'borrowed' experience being passed off as direct experience.

It was only after Independence that some educated Dalits in Odisha raised their voices in protest. Govind Chandra Seth, Santanu Kumar Das, Jagannath Malik, Kanhu Malik, and Kanduri Malik came together to set up the Dalit Jati Sangha (Dalit League) in 1953. Ambedkar, who was alive then, was a great source of inspiration for this Sangha, which tried to bring Dalit communities together to fight caste-related exploitations. Since many of these leaders were also creative writers they tried to bring awareness among Dalits through literary pieces. For example, Govind Chandra Seth wrote a biography of Ambedkar that instantly gained popularity. Santanu Kumar Das seems to have written four novels on caste inequalities and social injustices. The titles of the novels are *Aawhana* (A Call), *Vitamati* (Homestead), *Sania*, and *Pheria* (Comeback). None of these novels is traceable now. Many other Dalit leaders also started writing literature dealing with caste issues.

Radicalization of Dalit subjectivity

It was only around the 1970s and the 1980s that Dalits of Odisha began asserting themselves, if not organizationally at least individually through their writings which constituted 'Dalit literature' proper. This is seen as the third phase of protest, which took its inspiration from the modern world view underlying the central importance of freedom and equality. Writers of this new literature are but few. Most of them are teachers, lawyers, doctors, and government employees, constituting a small vanguard and symbolizing the advanced consciousness of a very backward and divided people. However, a look at the whole spectrum of Odia Dalit writers reveals a vision that goes beyond their geographical boundary and is relevant in any part of the world.

Bichitranand Nayak can be called a pioneer in Odia Dalit writings. In 1972 he published a collection of poems titled *Anirbana* (Liberation) using the term 'Dalit'. Like Nayak, poets and writers like Jagannath Malik, Krushna Charan Behera, Gobind Chandra Seth, and Ramachandra Sethi exposed the hypocrisies of the upper-caste Odia society. Jagannath Malik is well known for his novel *Kshudhita Kharavela* (The Hungry Kharavela), where he takes a dig at the historical character of Kharavela (a medieval Odia king) to interpret contemporary issues. Without naming anyone, through the novel he scrutinizes a modern politician, probably a chief minister of Odisha, who is both corrupt and autocratic. Malik's second important work is *The Ramayana*, where he reinterprets the episodic events of the epic from a Dalit point of view. He considers Ram an Aryan king, who goes to the jungle in order to teach the Adivasis and Dalits a lesson.

Krushna Charan Behera, Gobind Chandra Seth, and Ramachandra Sethi wrote on themes of untouchability, caste exploitation, gender inequality, and class oppression, and tried to bring Dalit discourse into the arena of Odia literature in a limited way. However, it was the Ambedkar Centenary Celebration in 1991 that motivated a number of Odia Dalit poets and writers to write their own histories. Accordingly, many educated Odia Dalits openly wrote about various facets of caste, class, and gender exploitations in Odia society. Among several poets and writers we can name Basudeb Sunani, Samir Ranjan, Sanjay Bag, Gopinath Bag, Dolamani Kandher, Pitambar Tarai, Ramesh Malik, Chandrakant Malik, Kumaramani Tanti, Supriya Malik, Basant Malik, Akhila Naik, Anjubala Jena, Mohan Jena, Samuel Dani, Anand Mahanand, Panchanan Dalei, and Pravakar Palka.

Poverty, powerlessness, untouchability, hypocrisy, and corrupt social practices have generated a variety of responses from
Odia Dalit writers. These responses are forms of protest aimed
at bringing about change through a social revolution. Their
protest is not against any individual or group but against society as a whole. They reject the so-called tradition, which helps
upper castes to legitimize the existing structures of inequality. Thus, Odia Dalit literature in all its forms interrogates
the world view and institutions of upper castes, and demands
a new social philosophy and practice based on these changes.
Akhila's Naik's *Bheda* has to be read against this background.
Let us see how the novelist explores caste questions and initi-
ates a dialogue among different constituencies of Odia caste
society on the issue of social justice.

The title of the novel

Akhila Naik's *Bheda* is considered to be the first Odia Dalit
novel which came out after a long silent spell. None of the previous novels by Dalits is currently available. It is a very short novel
of eighty-eight pages, comprising seven chapters, each named
after a character. In every chapter the novelist deftly addresses
caste questions. Before we critically analyse the novel let us
understand the etymological meaning of the title of the novel.

The word *bheda* has multiple meanings. The primary meaning is 'a sense of difference'. If bheda is used with another word
bhaba, it implies the differences that exist among people in
terms of caste, class, or race. In the Indian context *bhedabhaba*
basically denotes various kinds of caste discriminations that
the upper castes practise against the lower castes, especially
Dalits. Bheda also means 'the target'. In the novel Dalits are the

target of the upper castes because, after availing themselves of modern education, educated Dalits are now mobilizing resistance to protest against the monopolies of the upper castes. 'Bheda' also has another meaning: to properly understand the 'intricacies' of an incident or a happening. Thus, all the different meanings of the word are in some way or the other connected to the idea of caste and its corollary meaning, which is, caste discrimination followed by atrocities. By giving this powerful title to his novel Naik wants to draw our attention to how complex the caste situation is in Indian society. He openly condemns the caste system, which perpetuates caste atrocities. Finally, by writing this novel, Naik is able to initiate a dialogue on the question of human rights and social justice in a backward state like Odisha, where such issues are rarely raised in the public domain.

Narrative strategies

Naik's novel is a departure from the innumerable non-Dalit novels available in the Odia language. It seems as if Naik is experimenting with form, content, language, and grammar, all at the same time, in the novel. Even though it is a short novel Naik's narrative strategies enable him to deal with caste questions in all their complexities. Because of the simple narrative structure it has a free flow, and the author strategically uses the folk style to narrate his story. His characters debate many social issues before coming to certain conclusions. He narrates incidents in such a lively way that the readers feel they are witnessing first-hand events unfolding before them. He allows his characters to speak for themselves. Not surprisingly his language is free from the over-Sanskritized, standard

Odia register. He uses common people's language to narrate the events. As a result many of the idioms and phrases used by the villagers of Kalahandi region find their way into the text and enrich it. The novel thus expounds a new aesthetic.

As stated earlier the seven chapters are named after characters of the novel. They are Dinamastre, the school headmaster; Baya, the mad lawyer; Laltu, a young Dalit activist; Semi Seth, the businessman; Muna, a school-dropout Dalit who runs a tailoring shop; Mastrani, the headmaster's wife; and Santosh Panda, the local newspaper correspondent. These are but a few representative characters from 'small India', and yet they are an active component of a dynamic modern Indian state, participating in the process of nation building. Some of them, as we will see later, will sacrifice everything for this cause, whereas others will try to grab a large slice of the 'national cake'. Naik presents this national drama quite successfully, which ends in tragedy with Dalits suffering at the hands of upper-caste hooligans.

Largely the action of the novel takes place in some remote villages of Kalahandi district in western Odisha. Towards the end of the novel the action shifts from villages to the district headquarters of Kalahandi, that is, Bhawanipatna, the centre of power and authority. Naik draws attention to this link between the village and the town, perhaps to make a point: Where should Dalits live? This reminds us of Ambedkar's call to Dalits to leave villages and go to cities because Indian villages, beset by caste practices, are hellish. In cities Dalits will at least live in anonymity. Ambedkar's call is in contrast to Mohandas Karamchand Gandhi's idea of Gram Swaraj, where he finds peace and harmony among the villagers irrespective of their caste or class affiliations. In the novel Dalits in rural India have hardly any freedom and security. Without material means and opportunities they continue to stay on, although choosing to organize protests against the monopolies of the upper castes in their villages. The result is that they face severe atrocities. Their houses and shops are burnt down by the upper-caste mobs, leaving them without help or hope. They are rendered homeless in their homeland. Their leader, Laltu, is implicated in a false case by upper castes and is arrested. What are Dalits to do? Where can they go? What stakes have they in the Republic of India? Perhaps the novelist intends to ask these and many more such questions while narrating his stories of gruesome caste violence.

The novel was published in 2010 when India celebrated the sixtieth year of being a republic. Six decades of welfare policies with equity and justice enshrined in the Indian Constitution should have been enough to eliminate poverty, illiteracy, malnutrition, and all ills from India. But that did not happen. The novel takes us to Kalahandi, one of the poorest districts of India, to narrate its encounter with the development discourse.

The development discourse

Kalahandi came to the limelight in the 1980s when national dailies carried reports of starvation deaths and the sale of children. The news attracted the attention of the then prime minister of India, Rajiv Gandhi, who rushed to Kalahandi. Since then Kalahandi has earned negative fame for poverty, drought, famine, child selling, and malnutrition. The district has often been described by the media as the 'Somalia of India'. However, the ground reality is altogether different. After intense research several social scientists have informed us that the poverty we see in Kalahandi is more man-made than a calamitous phenomenon of nature. In the past Kalahandi was rich in natural resources and 60 per cent of its area was covered by dense forest.

The 1950s and the 1960s were the times when India went through a series of changes under the leadership of Jawaharlal Nehru. The welfare policies which Nehru propounded and propagated during his premiership were supposed to usher in 'development' in all spheres. But that did not happen in Kalahandi. Instead, in the name of development 'the worst' came to the Kalahandi region. Ironically when India was, after a decade of Independence, basking in the glory of freedom the people of Kalahandi witnessed hundreds and thousands of trucks plying day and night on its rough and uneven roads. People still describe the scene with awe about how these trucks carried away all the valuable wood—including teak—from their deep, green jungles. This well-organized looting was done by builders, contractors, bureaucrats, and politicians. Kalahandi, they thought, was a 'gold mine' and they extracted as much wealth as they could amass for themselves. They stripped Kalahandi of its greenery and left it barren and useless.

Apart from frequent droughts and famines Kalahandi has massive structural inequalities that directly affect the Dalits and Adivasis, who together constitute about 50 per cent of the population in the region. Being a resident of Kalahandi the novelist is an insider, who has witnessed these development narratives of the region. Therefore, his fictional accounts can be interpreted as an attempt to rewrite the social history of Kalahandi with a special focus on Dalits.

Education as emancipation

Naik begins his novel by highlighting the significance of education in Dalit lives. His character Dinabandhu Duria or Dinamastre is a primary schoolteacher who is a Dalit. For a Dalit to become a schoolteacher in Kalahandi is a great achievement as such an opportunity comes but rarely to the members of marginalized communities. In the meantime there is no doubt that Dalits in Kalahandi have occupied several government posts, thanks to modern education and the implementation of the reservation policy. But if we look at the ground realities it seems impossible for Dalits to get jobs in places where the upper castes have occupied positions for several years. Gauging the ways by which the upper castes have maintained their caste networks over the years, it would appear impossible for a poor Dalit like Dinamastre to get a job. But modern education has made a difference. Several social changes have made it possible for Dalits to find a place in upper-caste bastions and change the long-established power structure. It is for this reason that a tension is reflected throughout the narrative. Naik is very blunt in revealing the discourse of power in the novel. He provides several instances of how the upper castes feel threatened whenever a Dalit occupies any kind of a formal position. Naik traces this symptom to their 'caste mindedness', which makes the upper castes think that every public institution in India is their private property. However, Dinamastre's new job brings him opportunities as well as challenges. His job gives him the kind of economic security which his father and forefathers could never dream of. As a teacher he also earns respect in society unlike the other members of his community. He is a dedicated teacher, and after several years of struggle and hard work in public life he is now the headmaster of the primary school of his village, Firozpur. He is a simple, honest man.

It is through Dinamastre that Naik begins his caste discourse in the novel. As a Dalit writer and someone who has benefitted from modern education like Dinamastre, Naik, a teacher in the government college at Bhawanipatna in Kalahandi, believes that ultimately education will free Dalits from the bondage of caste slavery. This is a significant political stand because education has remained the main agenda of Dalit movements and has been advocated by Jotiba Phule and B.R. Ambedkar, as well as by present-day Dalit activists. Naik, while applauding the role of modern education for the Dalit emancipation project, also notices several cracks and fissures responsible for upsetting, and finally demolishing, such a noble project. Because of Dinamastre's Dalit background (he belongs to the Dom community), he is often mercilessly humiliated by his upper-caste counterparts. In the first chapter Naik describes how the school inspector, a highly educated Brahmin, deliberately uses his caste name when he addresses him in the presence of his students just to insult him. Occasionally the other upper castes also do the same. Dinamastre, for his part, internalizes such caste prejudices for the sake of his family. Fearing a backlash he never retaliates. His foremost aim in life is to raise his only son Laltu in a peaceful environment and to give him the best education possible. Contrary to his dreams Laltu abandons his education halfway and becomes a full-time social activist. He mobilizes the Dalits and the lower castes to resist the monopoly of the upper castes and becomes a celebrated leader of the cause. At the end of the novel he goes to jail after being implicated in a false case by the upper castes.

By creating a marked contrast between father and son, Naik hints at the radical side of Dalit politics. He critically evaluates the role of education: employment and social revolution. While the first is limited to the individual, or at best to the immediate family, the second extends to the community or society. Naik thus defines the role of education not in any abstract term but in the actual role it plays in society. Therefore, we see that when Laltu grows up he becomes conscious of the plight of his community members. He realizes that for no fault of theirs they are treated like animals by the caste-divided society. This realization makes him a rebel. As a leader he is not militant but works hard to change the mindset of the people. To begin a social revolution he organizes the youth of his area and his team guards the interests of the ordinary people. Apart from fighting against the hegemony of the upper castes they also fight corrupt officials, local contractors, politicians, and businessmen. Their activism brings a few visible changes to the region. For example, they guard the local forest when they realize that the local businessman Semi Seth is exporting truckloads of wood illegally. It is when they seize his tractor and report to the higher authorities of the forest department that Seth's loot comes to an end. This is but one example when the team works day and night to guard the larger interests of the people. Unfortunately their activism comes to an abrupt end when the upper-caste leaders unite to take revenge. Dalits are beaten up by the upper castes, their *basti*s are burnt down, and they are forced to desert their homes to save their lives, all with the police force passively standing by. Semi Seth, the Marwadi, and Banabihari Tripathy, the mad lawyer, both take the lead in organizing this carnage. The bribed police force naturally supports the upper castes.

The insider–outsider dynamic

Naik brings alive the insider–outsider dynamic through the two characters of Semi Seth and Banabihari Tripathy. While Laltu is an insider, the original inhabitant of the land, both Seth and Tripathy are outsiders. Naik collects information from local history and folklore to establish the 'foreign' origin of these two. Semi Seth's father Pawan Agrawal, a Marwadi, comes empty-handed to Kalahandi from Rajasthan. He opens a small ration shop in the village of Beheda and in no time amasses wealth illegally. After his father's death Semi Seth inherits his property and works through dubious means to further extend his empire. Among his possessions are a rice mill and a fleet of tractors, which ply day and night, taking away the best wood from the pristine jungles of Kalahandi. Semi Seth also buys food grains and forest products from the villagers at cheap rates and sells them at high prices. Even during droughts and famines his godown is never empty. It may be important to note here that Marwadis had spread their business in every nook and corner of Odisha. When the locals borrowed money from the Marwadis they did so knowing that they will have to pay a high rate of interest. In the 1980s the young people of Kalahandi organized movements to evict Marwadis from the region. Several riots took place in different towns and villages. But, eventually, the Marwadis stayed on after a peace treaty was signed between the two groups.

Banabihari Tripathy's ancestors come from Uttar Pradesh. In precolonial times Odisha had no Brahmin population, and Kalahandi was dominated by Adivasis, Dalits, and backward castes. Almost all the *gauntia*s were either Adivasi, or backward-caste people. Indeed the king of Kalahandi was an Adivasi.

With the Hinduization of the Kalahandi region, it seems, Banabihari's grandfather became a temple priest. He, however, tries to educate his son Sachikant Tripathy, who later becomes a forester in Junagarh in the Kalahandi region. Sachikant makes friends with Lochan Hati, the gauntia of Firozpur village, who belongs to a backward community (Other Backward Classes in today's context) called Gauda. Later Sachikant uses a trick to become the gauntia himself by replacing Hati. Banabihari goes off to Calcutta to study law and becomes a lawyer.

Semi Seth and Banabihari Tripathy join hands to further their interests. With the Hindutva movement spreading all over India in the 1980s and 1990s, these two gentlemen become the self-styled protectors of Hinduism. They organize the Rashtriya Swayamsevak Sangh *shakha*s in the villages and join in the hate campaign against Muslims and Christians. Opposed to any kind of conversion, they mobilize Dalits, Adivasis, and backward castes to join their campaign. When Laltu starts his activism they find a tough opponent in him, and initially try to harass him. But when Laltu resists successfully with the support of the people they plan to teach him a lesson. They not only implicate him in a false case and send him to jail but also organize mobs to perpetuate violence against the Dalits.

As mentioned earlier the ending of the novel is tragic. Laltu starts writing articles on the different problems in his region in order to bring them to the notice of a larger public. In appreciation of his wholehearted devotion to the cause of the people Santosh Panda, a Brahmin correspondent of the local newspaper *Hastakshep* (Intervention), recruits him as a local reporter. Panda assumes the role of a patron and supports Laltu's activism. But when a false case is filed against Laltu with the accusation that he mobilized Dalits to throw the bone of a cow into the temple, Panda suspects Laltu's integrity. Laltu tries his best to prove his innocence but Panda is not convinced. He remembers that Laltu had argued during their discussion that the upper castes, including Brahmins, ate beef during Vedic times and after. Though the correspondent promises help to Laltu he succumbs to the pressure of his caste prejudice. Panda not only supports his upper-caste brethren in the fight against Dalits but also sees to it that Laltu's arrest appears as front-page news to publicize his 'misdeeds'.

Panda's diabolic role to destroy the Dalit movement is not unusual. We know that the Indian media is, by and large, anti-Dalit. This leads Naik to comment that everyone is against Dalits: civil society, the state, the police, and the media. Social scientists will support Naik's argument. Vidya Devi, for example, who has researched caste-based discrimination, writes: 'Hindus control the government, the police, the judiciary, press and all else, including the military. Whenever there is any violence against Untouchables, the whole world comes down on them' (2008: 125). Unfortunately this is an Indian reality. Whenever and wherever Dalit atrocities have taken place the entire civil society has been up against Dalits accusing them instead of viewing them as the victims and helping them. This shows how deeply the idea of caste has penetrated the minds of the upper castes from where there is no escape. On account of Dalit atrocities in Odisha there are at least two fascinating tales told from the upper-caste perspective: one is Gopinath Mohanty's novel *Harijan* (1948), and the other is Basant Satpathy's short story '*Unnati*' (Development; 1972). While Mohanty expresses pity and sympathy towards his Dalit characters, Satpathy is more nuanced about depicting Dalit subjectivity. Here one can think about who qualifies to be a 'caste ally' in the Dalit movement.

Gender issue

Naik raises the gender issue in *Bheda* through Mastrani, Dinamastre's wife and Laltu's mother. As a Dalit woman she represents her class in the novel. But compared to many poor Dalit women of her neighbourhood who work hard for their survival, Mastrani does not have to work for a living. Being financially secure she commands both power and social position for which the other members of the community respect her. Even though she takes pride in Dalit culture she imitates upper-caste lifestyles by observing religious fasts and visiting Hindu temples. A charitable woman, she gives alms to beggars and mendicants and helps the poor and destitute.

Naik points out how Dalit patriarchy works to the advantage of Dalit men. Even though Mastrani is literate she sacrifices her career by prioritizing her family. She shares Dinamastre's dream of seeing Laltu in a respected position. Laltu's inability to complete his education and his failure to get a good job makes Mastrani very unhappy. But throughout his activism she supports him wholeheartedly. When he comes home late at night he finds her waiting for him. If he is unable to come back she stays up all night worrying. Thus, when Laltu sacrifices his career for his community and society, it is Mastrani who sustains his dream by sacrificing her time and energy to see a new society without caste discrimination.

It is through Mastrani that the author sheds light on the religious life of the Dalit community in the Kalahandi district of Odisha. Dalit communities across the district had been worshipping Budharaja, Dokribudhi, Thutimaili, Kalisundri, and such others since time immemorial. But once the upper castes, particularly the Brahmins, started coming and settling down in the areas they started building temples and worshipping their Hindu gods and goddesses such as Shiva, Durga, Ram, Krishna, and others. The local people, by imitating them, started worshipping these new deities. Thus, with the process of Hinduization and Brahminization the area flooded with Hindu gods and goddesses. This is precisely what happens in the novel. After an education, a government job, and economic security, Dinamastre's family starts worshipping Hindu deities—Mahadev in particular—which the illiterate villagers dislike. There is a debate in the novel between Majhi Baba, an Adivasi, who is also the village priest, and Dinamastre as to which gods and goddesses the villagers should worship. While Majhi Baba argues for worshipping only folk deities, Dinamastre offers justification to worship Hindu gods and goddesses along with folk deities. Since women are the custodians of culture it is through Mastrani that we get to know about the Hinduization of Dalit culture. Mastrani in her day-to-day life imitates upper castes. She bathes early in the morning, worships her deities, observes fasts, and visits temples, much to the satisfaction of the upper-caste people. Mastrani, by imitating the everyday life of the upper castes, thinks that she will be accepted as one among them. But that she was mistaken she discovers later.

Unlike Mastrani, Laltu is an agnostic. He criticizes his mother when she drags him to a temple. He challenges the existence of God when Mastrani tries to convince him of the significance of visiting temples. He cites many instances from the Puranas, shastras, and everyday life to tell her how Hinduism as a religion discriminates against Dalits. This she finally realizes when she visits the Mahadev temple in her neighbouring village. She cannot offer worship to the deity like others from the upper castes do. She can offer her puja only through the Brahmin temple priest. Disturbed, she questions herself: Is a Dalit not a human being? Though she realizes that the caste system is a discriminatory provision made by the upper-caste Hindus against Dalits, she points no accusatory fingers at upper-caste Hindus to correct their behaviour. Of course she is not an activist like her son. Naik, thus, portrays Mastrani not as a revolutionary Dalit woman but as a devoted wife and a loving mother who places her family before anything else.

♦

Bheda is undoubtedly a moving document on caste oppression. As we have seen Naik exposes the double standards of Indian caste-based society by highlighting the different forms of atrocities perpetrated by the upper castes on Dalits. Naik suggests that the idea of caste is enmeshed with violence, and violence in any form has to be condemned unequivocally by every member of civil society. Therefore, he has exposed the roles of various agencies of the Indian nation state—including the police, administration, education system, and media— which go hand in hand with the upper castes and become a part of the problem. Apart from the caste question Naik also raises important issues such as the role of caste and conversion, the role of the media and ecology, and development for debate and discussion. By doing so he, as a Dalit writer, urges his readers to at least reflect on them. This is what Dalit aesthetics is all about. As Sharankumar Limbale writes: 'The aesthetics of Dalit literature rests on: first, the artists' social commitment; second, the life-affirming values present in the artistic creation[;] and third, the ability to raise the reader's consciousness of fundamental values like equality, freedom, justice and fraternity' (2010: 120). It will not be an exaggeration to say that Akhila Naik in *Bheda* has successfully treated all three aspects of Dalit literature that Limbale has referred to.

Ernst Fischer in his book *The Necessity of Art* wrote that the purpose of art or literature cannot be merely aesthetic; there has to be a certain moral and social concern also. Though writers cannot always actually bring about changes in society, they can at least help create awareness. Even if they cannot offer a solution to problems they can at least diagnose the disease. Evaluating aspects of the British novel, Avrom Fleishman (1978: 13) has this to say on the function of literature:

> Literature supplements not only the primary cultural world of language, belief, and behavior but second-level systems as well, which like it attempt to discourse of those discourses. As in the human sciences, which have been shown to operate by conceptual schemes tantamount to fictions, the role of literary fictions is to locate us in our human world, to contrive for us a securer perch in reality by all the arts at its disposal. To determine how literature does this, by comparison with the fictions by which the human sciences confront reality, will help us toward the special virtue of fiction as a genre, toward its supplementary and invaluable contribution to the cultural world....

Thus, literature goes beyond being a historical record; it is an imaginative representation of human experience and, so long as it has the power to question our unthinking assumptions, it has contributed to the human cause. Dalit writers like Akhila Naik certainly belong to this school of thought.

Bibliography

Currie, Bob. 2000. *The Politics of Hunger in India: A Study of Democracy, Governance and Kalahandi's Poverty*. London: Macmillan Press Ltd.

Dash, Anup Kumar and Raj Kumar. 1994. 'A Study on the Implementation of the PCR Act in Orissa', report. Bhubaneswar: National Institute of Social Work and Social Sciences.

Deo, Fanindam and Padmalochan Barma. 1997. 'Roots of Poverty: Historical Context in Kalahandi, Orissa', unpublished report.

Devi, Vidya. 2008. *Dalit and Social Justice*. New Delhi: MD Publications.

Fischer, Ernst. 2010 [1963]. *The Necessity of Art: A Marxist Approach*. London: Verso Books.

Fleishman, Avrom. 1978. *Fiction and the Ways of Knowing: Essays on British Novels*. Austin: The University of Texas Press.

Forrester, Duncan B. 1980. *Caste and Christianity: Attitudes and Policies on Caste of Anglo-Saxon Protestant Missionaries in India*. London: Curzon Press.

Freeman, James M. 1978. *Untouchable: An Indian Life History*. London: George Allen and Unwin.

Gajarawala, Toral Jatin. 2013. *Untouchable Fictions: Literary Realism and the Crisis of Caste*. New York: Fordham University Press.

Galanter, Marc. 1984. *Competing Equalities: Law and the Backward Classes in India*. New Delhi: Oxford University Press.

Ganguly, Debjani. 2005. *Caste and Dalit Lifeworlds: Postcolonial Perspectives*. New Delhi: Orient Longman.

Kumar, Raj. 2010. *Dalit Personal Narratives: Reading Caste, Nation, and Identity*. New Delhi: Orient BlackSwan.

Limbale, Sharankumar. 2010. *Towards an Aesthetic of Dalit Literature: History, Controversies and Consideration*, translated from Marathi by Alok Mukherjee. New Delhi: Orient BlackSwan.

Mallik, Basanta Kumar. 2004. *Paradigms of Dissent and Protest: Social Movements in Eastern India, c. AD 1400–1700.* New Delhi: Manohar Publishers and Distributors.

Mansinha, Mayadhar. 1962. *History of Oriya Literature.* New Delhi: Sahitya Akademi.

Mishra, Narayan. 2004. *Exploitation and Atrocities on the Dalits in India.* Delhi: Kalpaz Publications.

Mohanty, Gopinath. 1994 [1950]. *Harijan.* Cuttack: Vidyapuri.

Mohanty, Janaki Ballabh. 1988. *An Approach to Oriya Literature: An Historical Study.* Bhubaneswar: Panchashila.

Mohanty, Jatindra Mohan. 2006. *History of Oriya Literature.* Bhubaneswar: Vidya.

Mohanty, Nivedita. 1982. *Oriya Nationalism: Quest for a United Orissa, 1866–1956.* New Delhi: Manohar Publishers and Distributors.

Naik, Akhila. 2010. *Bheda.* Bhubaneswar: Duduly Prakashani.

Naval, T.R. 2004. *Legally Combating Atrocities on Scheduled Castes and Scheduled Tribes.* New Delhi: Concept Publishing Company.

Nayak, R.K. 1984. 'A Study on the Problems of Untouchability with Emphasis on the Incidents of the Atrocities on Harijans in Orissa', report. Bhubaneswar: National Institute of Social Work and Social Sciences.

O'Hanlon, Rosalind. 1985. *Caste, Conflict and Ideology: Mahatma Jotirao Phule and Low Caste Protest in Nineteenth-century Western India.* London: Cambridge University Press.

Omvedt, Gail. 1996. 'Worst in a Hundred Years: The Kalahandi Drought', *Manushi*, 97 (November–December): 22–31.

———. 2011. *Understanding Caste: From Buddha to Ambedkar and Beyond.* New Delhi: Orient BlackSwan.

Pati, Biswamoy. 1999. 'Environment and Social History: Kalahandi, 1800–1950', *Environment and History*, 5 (3): 345–59.

Pradhan, Jagdish. 1993. 'The Distorted Kalahandi and a Strategy for Its Development', *Social Action*, 43 (3): 295–311.

Rao, Anupama. 2009. *The Caste Question: Dalits and the Politics of Modern Time*. Delhi: Permanent Black.

Samal, Kishor C. 1994. 'Drought and Its Toll in Kalahandi', *Mainstream*, 32 (14): 24–36.

Satpathy, Basant Kumar. 2013. 'Unnati', in Bikram K. Das (ed.), *The One-Eyed Chick and Other Stories*, pp. 108–18.

Satpathy, Sumanyu. 2009. *Reading Literary Culture: Perspectives from Orissa*. New Delhi: Rawat Publications.

Sen, Amartya. 2005. *The Argumentative Indian: Writings on Indian History, Culture and Identity*. New Delhi: Penguin Books.

Teltumbde, Anand. 2009. 'Understanding Existential Castes through Atrocity Metrics', available at http://www.countercurrents.org/teltumbde141109.htm (accessed on 30 January 2016).

Tripathy, Rebati Ballav. 1994. *Dalits: A Sub-human Society*. New Delhi: Ashish Publishing House.

Viswanathan, Gauri. 1998. *Outside the Fold: Conversion, Modernity, and Belief*. New Delhi: Oxford University Press.

Zelliot, Eleanor. 1992. *From Untouchable to Dalit: Essays on the Ambedkar Movement*. New Delhi: Manohar Publishers and Distributors.

One

Dinamastre

———◁◦▷———

The other day quite suddenly the school inspector (SI) of Dharamgarh block, Panda Sir, reached Firozpur UP School. He inspected all the classes—from first to fifth—asking questions in each class. In standard one he tested the students on *matras*; in standard two, he asked questions about *panakia*; in standard three, he asked about addition, subtraction, division, and multiplication; while in standard four, he gave a dictation. To the students of the fifth standard he asked spellings of several English words. After having finished the question session he asked Niranjan, the cleverest and most intelligent student in class, 'Tell me, child, what is the name of your headmaster?'

The boy was speechless at first and then stared at the roof. He could not comprehend why an intelligent student like him was being asked such a simple question. Just a little while ago he had been able to spell several English words like apple, umbrella, aeroplane, elephant, tomorrow, and house correctly. So he could not fathom whether SI Sir was joking with him or doubting his intelligence by asking such a simple question.

His heart pounded wildly and tears rolled down his cheeks; his tongue felt gummy as if he had just eaten raw *tendu*s.

It seemed as if SI Sir understood his turmoil and, to calm him down, encouraged him by asking softly, 'Look, the person who is standing to my left is the headmaster of your school. Tell me now, what is his name?'

Niranjan, being the brightest student of the fifth standard, tried to control his fear, hesitation, and doubt, and, a little encouraged by SI Sir, nodded his head and said, 'Dina Sir.' With the utterance of the name he seemed to lose his self-confidence.

SI Sir smiled faintly and said, 'Very good, very good. Dina Sir is your headmaster. You are perfectly right. Now tell me, what is his *full* name?'

Hearing such praise and a question like that from SI Sir took not just Niranjan by surprise but even the president of the school management committee, Debanand Meher, who was eavesdropping on the entire question–answer session, was equally shocked. That a person like Dinamastre should have a full name of some sort was news to Debanand.

Although Dinamastre's full name was Dinabandhu Duria, the students of Firozpur UP School knew him only as Dina Sir. For the last twenty-five years or so all those who had studied in the school had known him as Dina Sir. Before that when he was in Pakhanaguda LP School for five years, there, too, he was known as Dina Sir. His students were from all parts of the region, and many of them had got married in time and become parents themselves. Their children had also become Dina Sir's students. So all these parents and their children addressed him by the same name: Dina Sir. Some of them might have even known that his full name was Dinabandhu Duria. But it was never a problem for them or for Dina Sir whether someone knew his full name. Their love and respect for him would always be the same even if they had known it.

But SI Sir's face turned sour when he saw Niranjan, the most intelligent student of standard five, unable to state Dinamastre's full name. To humiliate Dinamastre before his students he said, 'Students are unable to tell me your name. What kind of teaching are you imparting, O Mastre?'

Dinamastre wanted to say something but could not. His ears began to burn. His head reeled. His face darkened. His eyes filled up with tears.

With a sour face SI Sir returned to the school office followed by Dinamastre and Debanand.

The office had a wooden chair and a small table; on the table were boxes of chalk, dusters, and a few registers. Towards the left side of the chair lay a long wooden bench along the wall. There was a tin trunk at the other end of the bench, just behind the chair. Seated on the chair SI Sir asked, 'Is lunch ready?'

Before Dinamastre could speak Debanand replied, 'Yes sir. The advocate sir has been waiting for a long time to see you.'

'*Arre*! Not that....' SI Sir, while turning the pages of the attendance registers, looked at Dinamastre and said, 'If the midday meal is ready, announce the lunch break.'

Dinamastre was about to go to his assistant teacher Narahari to enquire whether *dalia* had already been cooked for the students when SI Sir looking up from the register asked, 'Mastre, for how many students has dalia been cooked today?'

'For everyone, sir,' Dinamastre answered meekly.

'What does that mean? Everyone means how many?' SI Sir asked as if he were conducting a cross-examination.

'Sir, we have a hundred-and-twenty-three students,' Dinamastre's voice was trembling.

'But your attendance registers say that only sixty-three students are present today,' said the SI, getting irritated. He had a blackberry-sized wart between his lip and chin. Perhaps it was due to the weight of his wart that his lower lip drooped. 'Eating away poor children's food? Is it your dharma? Who will forgive you? The entry in the attendance register is sixty-three, but the stock register says one-hundred-and-twenty-three. Are you fooling me? Thieving ... robbery ... you are teaching this to the students? Who appointed you as a teacher? ... Go and beat a drum,' SI Sir went on rebuking him.

This time, too, Dinamastre wanted to say something but could not. His eyes became moist and his nose started to run. In his thirty years of service no one had ever pointed a finger at him and had called him a thief or a robber. For the first time such words had been flung at him when he was innocent of any crime.

It was true that sixty-three students had come to school that day. It was also true that the stock register had a record of one-hundred-and-twenty-three students. But the cook Raghuama had been asked to prepare dalia for only sixty-three students. This did not mean that he, Dinamastre, was stealing the food meant for the children. He was not a thief. The truth was that in order to feed the poor children the government threw a few sacks of dalia. But where would the fuel come from to cook that dalia? Would the children miss their classes to fetch wood? Did the government supply the little gur or sugar that was added to the dalia or the fried chillies and onions that were sometimes mixed with the dalia? If he did not sell dalia, was he to buy these things from his own pocket? To get some money Dinamastre sold as much dalia as was needed to buy the required fuel, gur, oil, onions, chillies, and so on. Just because he himself could not do such tedious work, Narahari Sir managed everything.

After all this if someone said that Dinamastre was stealing the dalia, no one, not even his enemies, would believe it. And as far as he knew he did not have any enemies.

Dinamastre's anger rose; he was about to break down. He thought of using a few coarse words to teach SI Panda a lesson but did not. He was compelled to remain silent because he knew how Makarand, the schoolteacher, after retiring from Kenduguda School had been suffering. That helpless, old man, otherwise gentle, had been running to the block office every week. His pension papers had not been prepared because, it seemed, he had once shouted at a certain SI or DI on some official matter. God knew when it would be done. Dinamastre's retirement was approaching and, if he could wait for another two years, he would be safe.

Before the bell rang for the lunch break Markand, the advocate's *halia*, came to the school verandah and stood about shuffling his feet. Seeing him Debanand came out from the office quietly, talked to him in a whisper, and returning to the office said to SI Sir in an ingratiating tone, 'The Advocate Sir has sent a man, Sir....' SI Sir, rising from the chair, told Dinamastre in a commanding voice, 'See me when you come to the block office for your salary. Don't hide your face and go home without meeting me.'

SI Sir rode to the lawyer's house on his bicycle with Markand following him at a run. Baya Advocate's big boundary wall was on the other side of the road and the gate of the wall was directly in front of the school. The gate was so big that two bullock carts could simultaneously pass through it. In the compound was a two-storeyed building. From the school verandah Dinamastre mutely watched SI Sir cycling through the gateway. He had not recovered from the shock that he got a while ago and had, in fact, forgotten that Debanand was standing near him. Wiping the sweat from his face with the corner of his dhoti, he saw Debanand smiling; he felt as if he had received another slap. The smile seemed to say: *After years of cheating, today you got caught.*

Dinamastre turned his face. 'Believe me, Debanand....' His voice faltered.

'How can I believe, Mastre? I saw your misdeed with my own eyes. I also heard everything about you. We thought you were a good man. You *really* turned out to be a good man!' There was accusation in Debanand's voice.

'You do not understand....' The mastre wanted to tell Debanand the truth. Except for Debanand no other person had heard the talk between him and SI Sir. He wanted to tell him all the facts and end all doubts. But Debanand was not ready to listen to anything. He thought he had discovered the mastre's real character.

'What is there to explain? If you wanted to explain, why didn't you so to SI Sir? If you want to give an explanation, go and explain it to Baya Advocate. I am a stupid person.' There was both mockery and anger in Debanand's voice.

Before Dinamastre could tell him anything, Debanand hurriedly got down from the school verandah and left. Dinamastre saw him crossing the road and entering Baya Advocate's gate.

Dinamastre stood at the school verandah for a very long time without realizing it. Suddenly the bell announcing lunch break rang. Carrying their thalis and *tasni*s the children ran noisily towards the tube well. Now they would receive dalia for their midday meal.

Had it been another day, Dinamastre would have strolled between the two rows of children to inspect the distribution of dalia. The *savarna* children from Mali, Teli, Gond, and Gauda communities sat in one row, and the Dom and Ghasi children in the other. Raghuama, the cook, started distributing dalia to the savarna children. In the past, sometimes, the dalia would be over before it reached the Dom and Ghasi children. Dinamastre, therefore, had ruled that every child would get two ladles of dalia in the first round. Thereafter if there was any dalia left, it would be equally distributed.

But today Dinamastre had no interest in the dalia distribution. In fact he had no interest in anything at all. He was tired. He returned to the office and lay down on the bench.

Sounds from the playground reached him: children at play; Narahari Sir's shouts; creaks of the tube well. It seemed to him that the sounds were whirling in the air like dry leaves and approaching him from afar. He was exhausted, his eyelids felt heavy.

'Without informing us in advance how come SI Sir made a sudden visit, Dina Sir, why?' Narahari Sir entered the office.

Suddenly Dinamastre opened his eyes. He heard no sound from outside. Perhaps the distribution of dalia was over and the children had left for their homes. Dinamastre had not heard Narahari Sir's question properly. So instead of answering his question he asked, 'What did you say?' and signalling towards the chair he said, 'Please sit down.'

But Narahari Sir continued to stand. How could he sit on the headmaster's chair—the only chair in the school? So Dinamastre got up from the bench and sat on the chair.

Narahari Sir had not yet learnt about how Dinamastre had been humiliated by SI Sir in front of the students, and how he was accused of pilfering dalia from the school. Dinamastre first considered telling him everything but then thought better of it. He wanted to forget those two incidents. However much he tried, nothing but those two events occupied his mind. He began to feel uneasy and his heart was pounding.

'Perhaps SI Sir had informed Baya Advocate well in advance about his visit,' Narahari Sir remarked seated on the bench.

Dinamastre had no interest in continuing the conversation. He wanted to take a little rest by sitting alone and closing his eyes, and so he answered indifferently, 'Is it?'

'Otherwise how did they finish cooking for him before his arrival? When I asked Markand why was he there, he said, "I have come to invite SI Sir for lunch."' Narahari Sir said, trying to prove that he had guessed it rightly.

'O, yes!' Dinamastre was astonished. He was about to say something but stopped. He had not thought about it. Had Baya Advocate planned and invited the SI to humiliate him? Had he? It was possible. The advocate was a dishonest man and a hypocrite. Moreover, the advocate was a Tripathy and the SI a Panda; both Brahmins. They could even be related. So to take revenge on him, had Baya Advocate taken this crooked path? Debanand was a *behera* in the advocate's house. He was a behera only in name but was in practice a halia. He was the head of thirteen domestic servants in Baya Advocate's house. Debanand supervised them all. He decided which land was to be ploughed when; which land needed seedlings; who would summon the stockman to inject the buffalo that was limping because its hooves were cracked; who would transport cow dung to the field; and so on. He took these decisions and saw to it that everything was done smoothly. Was he not Baya's servant? Just for show Debanand had been made the president of the school management committee, whereas the real president was Baya Advocate. By deceiving everyone he had become the president. It was even rumoured that in the upcoming panchayat election he would nominate Debanand to contest for the post of sarpanch. If the advocate played his cards well Debanand might well become a sarpanch.

Did it mean that Baya Advocate had conspired against him to create trouble by inviting SI Panda? Dinamastre thought to himself. But was he guilty? What crime had he committed? Had he not tried his best to persuade his son Laltu not to fight Baya Advocate and his evil companion Semi Seth? But his son was as adamant as a madman. Laltu stuck to whatever he thought was right and paid no heed to others. However much you persuaded him, however much you requested him, however much you cursed him, he never budged from his decision. When you talked to him, he would listen silently. His submissive appearance might make you think that he would amend his life and follow a new path. But the next day Laltu would be just the same. If Dinamastre was humiliated today, it was because of his son's activism. Dinamastre was angry with Laltu but his son was no longer in his control. So what was the use of getting angry or sulking? Dinamastre looked helpless. He took a deep breath.

◆

Two

Baya the Mad Lawyer

◇

The mad lawyer Baya's real name was Banabihari Tripathy. To his face people called him Lawyer Sir but behind his back, everyone, whether young or old, called him Baya the Mad Lawyer. Even the halias of his house called him this. If you met any one of them on your way and asked where he was going, the answer would be, 'To the mad lawyer's house' or 'To the mad lawyer's field'.

Mind you, he was not called 'Mad Lawyer' critically or angrily. People knew him by that name and just that. Of course he had a streak of instability. He was extremely temperamental; he hardly spoke, and when he did it sounded as if he was shouting; when he made a request it was as if he was giving an order. In truth, no one had ever heard him making a request. He always ordered others and, when he did, it suited his expression perfectly.

When Baya was studying law at Calcutta his friends there used to call him a mad fellow. It had been several years since he had quit his law practise. No one even from the older generation was able to tell where and in which court he had practised before he gave it up because there was not a single court nearby.

If there was one, it might have been in Bhawanipatna, the headquarters of Kalahandi. But wasn't it well known that Bhawanipatna was ruled by a king and that he had his own durbar where the guilty were punished after trials? No one could tell whether or not the lawyers' arguments were even heard during the trials.

Of course there was hardly any dispute or murder or even theft in the villages at that time. Court cases, if any, were few and rare and even those were solved in the village itself. The *gana*, the gauntia, along with five other elderly gentlemen of the village used to discuss matters and pass judgement. Therefore, no one had even heard the term 'court'.

Some said that Baya practised law in Calcutta, while others said Cuttack. But everyone believed that he did not last long in his profession because of his cranky nature. Every court case results in either a defeat or a victory. If you lose today, tomorrow you may win; if you win today, tomorrow you may lose. This is the inevitable law of the world and so it has always been. But Baya could never accept defeat; he always wanted to win. It was said that once one of his clients lost a case and when that happened Baya came to believe that it was that 'bastard' judge who was biased. After the judge had read his verdict Baya pulled his hair, banged his head three or four times on the table, tore all the papers into pieces, and shouted like a madman.

The entire court was in an uproar.

Helpless, the judge banged the hammer on his table and tried to stop him. But who could control Baya's wrath? Furious, he slipped off a shoe and threw it at the judge. The shoe hit the judge and blood oozed from his nostrils. Some say the shoe hit the judge's ear and not the nose but it was his nose that bled.

Whoever was present in the court—the lawyers, the clients, the police, the peons—were all stunned. As they watched astounded Baya bent to take off his other shoe. Had it not been for the two hefty peons who instantly caught him, something worse would have followed.

After that incident Baya's licence to practise was cancelled. He distributed some belongings he had either in Calcutta or in Cuttack, left the others, and returned to his village empty-handed. Even if his licence was not cancelled Baya would have anyway come back to his village. How could a man of his stature who had so much dignity and self-respect continue his practise after losing a case? Above all, why did he have to be a lawyer?

After returning to the village Baya concentrated on farming. That did not, however, mean that he got up early, yoked his bullocks, and went out to plough. First of all, he was from a Brahmin family; secondly, he had studied law; thirdly, there was no shortage of domestic servants to plough his land. After breakfast and afternoon tea he used to go round the fields. That was all. The rest of his time was spent reading, not slim volumes like *Keshab Koili*, *Kapat Pasha*, or *Sitachori* but thick books, and listening to the radio. All other work such as calculating the profit and loss from agriculture, paying the workers, and looking after the guests was managed by the new gauntia.

The new gauntia was Baya's father, who did not do all the work alone. He had an accountant named Debaduta Mohanty to assist him. Debaduta was the younger brother of Baibasuta Mohanty. But they were not real brothers. Debaduta was the son of Baibasuta's father's third wife whom he had married at the age of fifty. So Baibasuta and Debaduta had the same father but different mothers. In fact it was Baibasuta who brought Debaduta to the new gauntia. The new gauntia and Baibasuta were friends, as both were working as foresters. Baibasuta was the forester of Churakhman jungle, which was on the other side of Junagarh. The new gauntia was the forester of Sahajkhol jungle located next to Beheda. How Baya's father and the forester of Sahajkhol jungle, Sachikant Tripathy, became the new gauntia of Firozpur village is also a story.

Lochan Hati had always been the gauntia of Firozpur village. He was a Gauda by caste. He owned three to four hundred acres of land, which meant he owned more than half the village. He had not studied much. During Lochan Hati's time, except the Brahmins and the Karans, the others hardly cared to study. In fact there was no need to study. It was sufficient if one just learnt to count. Lochan Hati had learnt that much. He also knew a few letters of the alphabet to mark his signature. People say that he was a gem of a person: sociable, simple, and true. He even used to call out to passers-by and enquire about their well-being. The small and poor farmers never felt that they were his tenants; they were like his sons and nephews.

Forester Sachikant Tripathy's own house was in Deojhar village, which was very close to Bhawanipatna. But Deojhar was not his ancestral village; his father Umakant Tripathy had come from one of the Brahmin *sasan*s situated on the bank of the river Baitarani in Jajpur. Kalahandi at one time did not have sufficient numbers of Brahmins for performing pujas, reading the Puranas, and performing *homa*s and yajnas. The king of Kalahandi had, therefore, invited Umakant to settle in his kingdom and had arranged land for his home and cultivation at Deojhar. But even Jajpur, it seems, was not the ancestral village of Umakant; his grandfather had come from either Varanasi or Lucknow. When Sachikant became the forester, he brought his parents, wife, and children and settled down in Deojhar village. He lived with them for most of the year except during his tour when he would go to the Sahajkhol jungle to oversee the cutting of trees. But his tours were never long. At best he would visit Dahagaon, Beheda, and Firozpur villages six or seven times in a year. Whenever he went on a tour he used to stay at Lochan Hati's home. It might be for a day or a half but he would surely stay with him.

Lochan Gauntia and Sachikant Forester enjoyed a very good relationship. They used to call each other *mita*. During times of need Sachikant used to lend money to the gauntia. The gauntia, on his part, helped Sachikant steal timber from Sahajkhol jungle by sending his halias and buffalo carts for free. Lochan Gauntia had twenty-two pairs of strong buffaloes. They carried the timber from Sahajkhol jungle to either Moter or Charbahal, or even as far as Mahichala.

There was a big mango grove between Charbahal and Mahichala with a hundred-and-thirty-three mango trees. Every year during the month of Pausha the dewan appointed by the king of Kalahandi used to camp there to collect revenue. Till the month of Magha the gauntias of the Kalahandi region used to collect revenue from their respective villages and reach the camp to deposit it on the given day.

That year the news was that the camp would start on the third day of the new moon night in the month of Magha. But since there was drought in Firozpur village Lochan Gauntia was extremely anxious. His tenants had no grain. They hardly managed a meal a day. Where would they get their revenue from? But the revenue had to be deposited. What could be done? Lochan Gauntia was in a fix.

Luckily on the first day of the new moon night in the month of Magha, Sachikant Forester arrived. At the sight of Sachikant the gauntia felt his life returning. After sharing his worries with Sachikant he said, 'You are the only hope during this difficult time. I promise to repay you with 50 per cent interest before the end of the coming harvesting season and will remain grateful to you forever.'

Assuring him that he would somehow arrange the money over the next two days and return, Sachikant left for Beheda that very day but never returned. Days passed, the first day, the second day, and even the third, but there was no sign of his return. Waiting anxiously for Sachikant, Lochan Hati's eyes went dry. Finally he lost hope.

Sachikant returned after a month, not as a forester or a friend of Lochan Gauntia but as the new gauntia of Firozpur village. Since Lochan Gauntia did not go to the revenue camp the dewan auctioned the post of gauntia of Firozpur. Having reached there in time, the forester Sachikant Tripathy won the bid. After a month he took possession of Firozpur village as the new gauntia. Thereafter people started calling Sachikant Forester, Baya's father, the new gauntia.

Earlier Lochan Hati used to smoke ganja occasionally. But after he lost the post of gauntia he began to smoke it more frequently. He smoked ganja so much that his cough was soon speckled with blood. When people learnt of it they said that his liver was full of holes. A certain physician suggested that if he ate the liver of a tiger fried in goat's ghee continuously for three *prahara*s the holes in his liver would fill up and he would be like a youth of sixteen.

The goat's ghee was arranged but, despite several attempts, there was no tiger's liver to be found. One day a trader, who used to carry salt in his bullock cart from Junagarh to Pawan Marwadi's godown at Beheda, said that he knew a forester named Baibasuta Mohanty who was an expert in killing tigers. He said that tigers could smell Mohanty from a distance and ran to save their lives mewing like cats and hid in holes or under stone covers. Mohanty, for his part, found and killed them.

After several requests to the salt trader he finally brought Mohanty Forester to Firozpur. The forester made a deal with Lochan Hati: if the old gauntia transferred ten acres of land to the forester he would bring the liver of a tiger within a week. The deal was sealed. After Lochan Hati lost the post of gauntia he was left with only seventeen acres of land of which ten acres were transferred in the name of Mohanty Forester. The deed was signed in front of the new gauntia. Unlike today in the past people did not take the trouble of going to the tehsil office. All kinds of land transactions—whether leasing, buying, or selling—were done on plain paper in the presence of the gauntia. The gauntia and two other gentlemen were required as witnesses. Thus, three persons were enough to complete a deed of sale.

After four days Mohanty Forester came to the old gauntia's house with the tiger's liver. The old gauntia fried it in goat's ghee and ate it continuously for three praharas. The night he finished eating the last dose of the liver he slept peacefully, not coughing even once. The next morning he should have got up like a young man of sixteen. But, unfortunately, he did not wake at all. His pulse had stopped. People in the house started crying. This should not have happened. How did it happen? Amidst the wails someone discovered a coiled pit viper sleeping under the mehndi shrub. No one had any doubt. It must have been a snake bite!

After two years the tiger-killer forester Baibasuta Mohanty returned to Firozpur with his younger brother Debaduta to claim those ten acres of land. Both of them went straight to the new gauntia's house. From that day onwards Debaduta Mohanty settled in Firozpur and became the new gauntia's accountant.

The same Debaduta Accountant supervised all the works of the new gauntia: jobs related to farming, servants, or guests. That was why Baya virtually had no work to do after he quit his practise and came back to the village. Throughout the day he either read big books or relaxed and listened to the radio. His only work was to go round the field after breakfast and after his evening tea.

But one day his daily field inspections came to an end. One morning, as usual, Baya set out on a round after having his paratha and milk. It had rained heavily all night. After walking a little distance on the ridge of the field Baya realized that his shoes were getting stuck in the squelchy mud. Layers of gummy mud got deposited under his shoes making them heavier. He tried to remove the mud by rubbing his shoes on the grass and tried to walk on but the problem continued. So he was compelled to take off his shoes and hold them. He had not walked even two steps when he cried, 'Oh, Ma!' and fell on the ridge. A thorn from the *gahera* tree had pierced his left foot.

In his whole life Baya had not once stepped on a thorn. He had also not stumbled on anything before. Not once had he ever hurt his hands or feet. His legs shook with pain. Tears rolled down his cheeks. Listening to his cries the halias ploughing in the nearby fields rushed towards him and asked concernedly what had happened. Baya was unable to say anything. He tried to balance himself on his elbows, bent over backwards, and was only able to raise his left leg.

A halia named Bhubane Gauda ran to the field and fetched some muddy water in his palms. He poured the water on Baya's left foot and cleaned the mud with the end of his towel, revealing the thorn that had pierced his foot. The moment Bhubane pulled out the thorn, blood oozed. At the sight of his own blood Baya's pain increased. Bile shot to his head. In frustration and rage he picked up one of his shoes and started beating the ground and shouted at the same time, 'You harlot, how dare you bite me! You prostitute, what insolence! I'll never look at your face.' The halias looked at him dumbfounded, suspecting that an evil spirit had possessed him. But after a while they were relieved when Baya calmed down and started limping homeward, muttering all the while.

Owing to Baya's obstinacy the entire two acres of double-cropping, fertile land was given to Bhubane Gauda. People say that there was another reason behind the transfer. It seems that Ketaki, who was employed in the new gauntia's household to clean utensils, got pregnant. When it became public she was already in her sixth month. Having no other way Ketaki was married off to Bhubane. The new gauntia bore all the expenses of the wedding feast. As if it were a normal marriage Ketaki was given a few clothes, utensils, and some jewellery. Bhubane was also given two acres of that fertile land as dowry. After three months Ketaki gave birth to a fair-skinned boy who bore a close resemblance to Baya. But no one can change another's destiny. The infant did not see his fifteenth sunrise.

Baya stopped going to the field after that and spent all his time reading or listening to the radio. He hardly needed to do anything for his family. His sons were both studying elsewhere. His household servants—both men and women—always said that the husband and wife were not on good terms. Apparently Baya regularly shouted at his wife, used obscene language, and even beat her making her sob all night. But her cries never reached beyond the high-boundary walls of their house. The gates on the boundary walls were locked from the inside at night and the house was set well away from the gates.

No one knows when Baya got interested in the activities of the shakha. When people started saying that the Christian missionaries had started visiting the Dompada of Jaitpur frequently, and that at least seven families there had decided to convert to Christianity, Baya started the shakha for the first time at Gheeapoda Ground adjacent to the Mahima Tungi at Jaitpur. The Mahima Tungi was also known as Tungi Gudi or Tungudi. Once a year on the full moon night in the month of Magha a fair was organized there. Millions of Alekha babas from every corner of India met in the field for this annual congregation. Throughout the night they beat tambours amidst shouts of *Mahima, Niranjan, Nirakar, Alekh, Alekh*. They also lit sacrificial fires and poured lots of ghee into it. So the ground was called Gheeapoda Ground.

So Baya started his first shakha in that Gheeapoda Ground. Before that nobody had any idea about what the shakha was and what was done there. The place was crowded with people who thronged from nearby places in and around Jaitpur. School children from Jaitpur, Beheda, Firozpur, Dahagaon, Thutibor, and nearby places assembled there. A bhai from Bijamara of Jaipatna area came to teach the children games such as Me Shivaji, Whose Kashmir, and Ram–Ravan. After these activities the meetings started but not before Danar Sahu, the gauntia of Jaitpur, and Baya delivered speeches.

People had heard many things about Baya but few had seen him. That day people got the opportunity to see him from close quarters. He wore a pure-white dhoti and a kurta set which looked like the feathers of a heron. He draped a silk scarf over his shoulder which was tinged with ochre. His father had passed away a few days ago, so his head was shaven. As the rays of the sun fell on him his smooth head and forehead shone like gold.

Baya declaimed, 'We all are Hindus. A Brahmin is a Hindu, a Dom is also a Hindu; Gond, Gauda, Mali, Teli—all are Hindus. All Hindus are brothers. Therefore, we must unite. The Christians and Muslims are foreigners who have come to our country to enslave our Hindu brothers. We the Hindus are the masters of this country. We should not be someone's servants; we should always be the masters. We should not convert either to Islam or Christianity; we should remain Hindus. Christians and Muslims are conspiring against us to take some of our brothers into their fold. If that happens our enemies will become stronger. If that happens the loss is surely ours. Shall we chop off our legs ourselves? No, never. I warn you, those brothers of ours who are becoming instruments in the hands of our enemies, are snakes in the grass. Lord Sri Krishna has stated in the Gita, it is better for a Hindu to die rather than become a Christian or a Muslim. It has been mentioned in the Bhagabata that people who change their religions go to hell after death. In hell the messengers of Yama skin and chop them into pieces and fry them in hot oil like *arisha* cake....'

Many children came to the shakha to play. The Gheeapoda Ground started vibrating with slogans such as *Aaram, Daksha, Agreshara*, and *Dwaja pranam*. Baya also made it a point to come to the shakha every Saturday to participate in the *boudhik barga* and to deliver speeches. The shakha continued smoothly for two to three years until something unexpected happened. A quarrel between Laltu, a Dom boy, and Yuvaraj, a Teli boy, over something minor resulted in a fight, leading to big trouble in the village, after which the parents did not allow their children to go to the shakha. The number of children attending the shakha dwindled, and it finally closed down. By then the Christian missionaries had also been prevented from visiting Jaitpur Dompada frequently.

◆

Three
Laltu

———◇———

Laltu had no personal enmity with Baya the Mad Lawyer because there was no reason to quarrel. How can there be a quarrel between two people if they share no relationship at all? Laltu and Baya had had nothing to do with each other in the past, nor would they in the present, nor was any expected in the near future. To think about their friendship was unimaginable; it was like trying to square a circle.

Baya was a Brahmin, the highest caste, whereas Laltu was a Dom, an untouchable. Succeeding his father Baya became the gauntia of Firozpur village and the owner of at least three hundred acres of land. One can say that even Kuber served under him. On the other hand, Laltu's father, Dinamastre, was an insignificant person with a meagre salary, a teacher in Firozpur Primary School. And his salary? Baya spent heftily on tea and snacks every week! The rest of his wealth was three acres and seven decimals of land which included his homestead. Of the total land, more than half was only in name, being sandy and stony. Not even *chakunda* trees could grow there. If you looked for soil you would not find even a handful.

Baya had studied law in Calcutta. Had he wanted he could have been a high-ranking officer living a comfortable life and travelling frequently by air. Of course he could fly even now, if he so desired. Laltu, on the other hand, was completing his senior secondary (plus two) in Government College, Bhawanipatna. But one could view him as a 'high-school fail' because he skipped the final examination.

Baya's sons were in high-ranking jobs outside the district. The elder one was the district judge of Phulbani; the younger one was the manager of the State Bank of India branch in Berhampur. On the other hand, after quitting his study, Laltu was seen roaming everywhere like a wandering ghost and could rightly be called a *bana*.

Therefore, there was no comparison between the two. They were poles apart. Why then should there be any quarrel between them?

But it did happen.

Not a verbal or a physical quarrel. It was a different sort of quarrel.

Like every other night members of the Sahajkhol Jungle Suraksha Committee were on guard at the Thutibor village crossing since midnight. They had seen five buffalo carts and a tractor going towards Sahajkhol jungle the previous evening. It was around the third quarter of the night when all the five buffalo carts returned one after another. Each cart was carrying a heavy wooden log between three to five feet long. The committee members jumped out from their hiding places on to the road and stopped all the five carts. The halias who were manning the carts panicked. They could not speak. After a lot of interrogation they finally revealed that they were working as halias in Bhaja Sahu's house, the cloth merchant of Dharamgarh.

The halias pleaded for their release but the committee members refused. They led the carts to Kartik Pota's backyard and unloaded the logs there. They unyoked the buffaloes and told the halias, 'Go and tell Bhaja Sahu that the members of the committee have seized his carts. Let him come and talk to us.'

Just then the headlights of a tractor flashed in the distance and everyone heard it approaching. The committee members ran to the crossroads and blocked the road with three big stones. The tractor halted. The trolley of the tractor was loaded with wooden planks. Upon closer inspection they recognized the driver: Manabodo Sori from Firozpur. After failing his matriculation examination from Beheda Danteswaree High School two years ago he was now driving Baya Lawyer's tractor.

No enquiry was necessary. None was made. The members knew immediately that the wooden planks belonged to Baya. Manabodo tried to scare the committee members away, 'With whose permission are you seizing this wood? If Baya comes to know, he will put you in the Dharamgarh jail. Leave now. Let me go.'

The members knew that Baya Lawyer was well connected. What could they do? Those who were timid said, 'Leave him.' But Kartik Pota, the secretary of the Sahajkhol Jungle Suraksha Committee, said, 'No, we will not let him go. Let Laltu come and then we will decide.'

Rame Jagat, who was admitted to Dharamgarh Panchayat College the previous year but had hardly attended college, and another boy named Dhania ran for half an hour and reached Laltu's village, Marichapadar.

Laltu was the president of the Sahajkhol Jungle Suraksha Committee. It had been his and Kartik's idea to set up such a committee. They became friends while they were at the

Danamuda Ashram School. Their friendship strengthened in the Sahajkhol jungle. Coming from Danamuda, after crossing Malgaon, one reaches the river Bori in the Sahajkhol jungle. One day, two furlongs from the river under a thick mahua tree, they had got frightened. Trembling, they had held each other tight. At that moment their friendship was sealed. Recalling that moment they still got goosebumps.

♦

Laltu studied from the fourth to the seventh class in Jaitpur Middle English School, standing first in class for three consecutive years. The teachers thought that he would pass the seventh class with at least an 'A' grade, if not an 'O'. His father repeatedly told him that if he passed with an 'O' grade he would admit him to the Brajmohan High School at Bhawanipatna.

But Laltu had taken a vow before Manjula that he would never go to Bhawanipatna even if his father cut him to pieces. Manjula was one of his best friends. She was slim and beautiful. She had a black mole on her left cheek, and whenever she smiled a dimple was near it. If Laltu secured the first position in the class, Manjula stood second. But Manjula was not jealous of Laltu. She used to bring guavas, berries, pickles, and other things for him from her home, hiding them in her school bag. Both of them had decided to study at Danteswaree High School after the seventh class.

It was for Manjula that Laltu fought Yuvaraj.

Yuvaraj was five years older than Laltu. After passing his matriculation examination he was studying in Bhawanipatna Government College. He had come to his village during summer vacations. Like other boys he, too, visited the shakha regularly. One day, after the shakha, Laltu and two other boys were returning to their village in the evening. On the way there was a tiny stream named Legrelega. The people of Marichapadar and Jaitpur depended entirely on this stream for washing and bathing. Laltu and the other two boys were about to reach the stream when Yuvaraj called Laltu from behind. Perhaps Yuvaraj and his friends had come to the stream to relieve themselves.

Laltu stopped. Yuvaraj took Laltu aside and, as if passing some secret, whispered in his ears, 'If you do something for me, I will give you five mangoes.' Laltu could not imagine what that errand could be for which Yuvaraj was bribing him with five mangoes.

The mango tree in the backyard of Yuvaraj's house used to bear mangoes that were different from others. While the ripened mangoes on other trees were yellow, the mangoes at Yuvaraj's house were red. People used to call them *sinderi*. Laltu had seen sinderi mangoes from far, but had not tasted them. His mouth watered at the mention of the mangoes.

'First tell me what you want me to do.'

'Don't tell anyone. There will be trouble if someone knows about it,' Yuvaraj whispered.

'No, I will not tell anyone, I promise,' Laltu was becoming impatient.

'Give this to Manjula,' Yuvaraj said taking out a piece of paper which was folded four times and placed it in Laltu's shirt pocket.

'What is it?' Laltu asked him, frightened.

'A letter.' Yuvaraj's smile flashed in the dark.

'A letter! Why?' Laltu was curious as well as surprised.

'You are a child. You won't understand. When I come to the shakha tomorrow I will bring mangoes for you,' Yuvaraj enticed him again.

When Laltu unfolded Yuvaraj's letter at home under the lantern light he understood that Yuvaraj had written something vulgar on it. On the paper Yuvaraj had scribbled *I love you* and below it, *Your lover, Yuvaraj.* Laltu had no doubt that 'love' was a vulgar term. He thought of taking the letter to the headmaster of his school to ensure punishment for Yuvaraj. But Yuvaraj did not study in their school; he studied in Bhawanipatna Government College. He was not sure if the headmaster would punish a grown-up boy. So he tore the paper and threw the pieces into the fire.

The next day when Laltu was on his way to the shakha his mind was buzzing. *Yuvaraj should not come to the shakha today ... Yuvaraj should suffer from fever today ... Yuvaraj should die today...!*

But Yuvaraj was already in the shakha and waiting for Laltu. Neither the head instructor of the shakha nor any other functionary had arrived yet. When Laltu told Yuvaraj that he had thrown the shredded letter into the fire, Yuvaraj punched him hard on his left cheek. Laltu was about to fall but managed to stay upright. The blow made him bleed from the mouth and his eyes got teary. When he stepped back to save himself his feet touched a stick to which the shakha's flag was tied. When Yuvaraj ran forward to hit him again Laltu swung the stick, brought it down hard over Yuvaraj's hand, and fled towards the village.

After dinner that night Dinamastre was reading something in the light of a lantern by his cot when some uproar broke out in his courtyard. 'You motherfucker Dom boy, come out of the house!' came a shout while someone thumped on the door. Dinamastre's heart hammered. Leaving the cooking pots and pans uncovered, Mastrani came running from the kitchen. They could not understand what had happened. Again shouts were raised in the yard, 'The motherfucker Doms, just because they have learnt a few letters they think they are up there … come out, you motherfucker…!' Once more there was loud pounding on the door.

Dinamastre asked, 'Who…? What has happened?'

'Nothing has happened. *Saala*, come out of your house….'

Lantern in hand, Dinamastre opened the door and stepped into the courtyard. There were about ten to fifteen people outside, each with a stick. Even in the dim light of the lantern Dinamastre recognized everyone. They all belonged to the Telipada of Jaitpur village.

An hour of arguments, counterarguments, and shouts followed.

Yuvaraj was a distant nephew of Danar Sahu, the gauntia of Jaitpur. The entire village was in an uproar when the news spread that Dinamastre's son, Laltu, had beaten Yuvaraj black and blue with a stick. How dare a Dom boy beat the gauntia's nephew? It needed a lot of courage! Immediately a meeting of the Teli Samaj was convened. Yuvaraj had to be brought back into the caste after his *suddhi*. But what about the pride of the Dom saalas which was growing by the day?

'If the Doms are not controlled now, a day will come when they will sit on our heads and rule us.'

'Go and break that saala's hands and legs,' ordered Danar Gauntia.

The crowd had come to execute Danar Gauntia's order. In spite of repeated pleas from everyone, they were quite adamant.

Their only demand was, 'Bring Laltu out of his house.' If they could not break his hand or leg that was fine. But should they go back to their village without beating or slapping him? Would not the pride of the Teli Samaj suffer? Today a Dom boy had beaten a Teli. Tomorrow these saalas would beat another ten Telis if the wickedness of the Doms was not controlled.

Dinamastre realized that the problem was building as fifteen to twenty young men from his community had come out holding lathis. If the situation lasted any longer there would be open clashes. He did not want such a meaningless event to lead to a caste war. So he asked for forgiveness with folded hands, 'Laltu is a child and does not know about caste. Forgive him. You all go back now. Tomorrow I will bring him along to meet the gauntia. Whatever his decision, we will obey.'

The next morning a panchayat was held at Jaitpur. There, too, Dinamastre begged for forgiveness. He requested the villagers not to continue the fight which the children had started. The gauntia said, 'It is all right Mastre but who will bear the expenses for Yuvaraj's suddhi rites to bring him back into the caste fold?'

How much would it cost to organize a feast for the community people? Sixty kilos of rice, eight kilos of dal, vegetables, oil, and spices—at least two hundred rupees. Dinamastre instantly handed over the money without bargaining.

After two days Laltu's friends, who had gone to the shakha, informed him that Yuvaraj was carrying the bone of a cow in his pocket to beat him. It seemed that he had told them, 'Tell him I had to shave my head for him. I shall have no peace till I force *him* to tonsure *his* head.' It was a belief that even the Doms lost caste if beaten with the bone of a cow. In order to come back to the community fold they had to tonsure their heads and sprinkle cow-dung water on themselves to retrieve their purity. On such occasions it was also a tradition to invite the community people to a feast.

Laltu did not go to the shakha again. After a few days it was heard that when Baya went to the shakha for the boudhik barga, the upper castes proposed to forbid Dom boys from participating in the shakha. But Baya did not agree with them. Instead he explained that if they were not permitted the Doms would become Christians and, if they did, the strength of Christians would go up. If the strength of the enemy increased, who would be the losers? Naturally the Hindus. Which group would be in danger? Obviously the Hindus. But the people did not like Baya's arguments and they stopped their children from going to the shakha. Although not all the children obeyed their parents immediately, eventually the attendance of the children in the shakha declined, and within a few months the shakha was closed.

◆

When the seventh standard board examination results were declared, Laltu had got only a 'C' grade. Scared of his father's beating Laltu entered the house to hide under the *bhadi*; it was very dark and stank of the excreta of cats and rats. He could hardly breathe. Laltu tolerated the ordeal for a long time. He heard his father saying, 'You have spoilt your son through overprotection. Now see the result.' There was a long silence. When he came out from his hiding and surreptitiously reached the verandah, he saw his father reading on a jute-woven cot and his mother sitting on the floor, silently separating stone particles from rice grains in a winnowing pan. The moment Laltu saw them he thought of turning back quickly but just then his father's gaze fell upon him. '*Kulangar*, black sheep!' his father muttered, as if to himself, and once again went back to reading his book.

After that, for nearly a week Dinamastre neither looked at Laltu nor talked to him. Laltu on his part tried to talk to him twice or thrice but received no response at all. Laltu felt like crying. His father who had once loved him so much and cared so tenderly for him was not even looking at him. Everything lost its charm. *I should have died*, he thought. His sense of guilt turned into melancholy.

One night during dinner Dinamastre suddenly announced that henceforth Laltu would study in Danamuda Ashram School. Laltu felt as if a thunderbolt had struck his head. That year among the students from Danamuda Ashram School who had appeared for the matriculate examination, three had got a first division, eight had secured a second division, and the rest had passed. So everyone was praising the school. But Laltu remembered Manjula's face and the promise he had made to her. He wanted to protest against his father's decision but, remembering the silence between them for a week, said nothing. If he refused to study at Danamuda School his father might never talk to him again.

But Laltu's mother protested immediately, 'Why? When there is a school at Beheda, close to home, why should my child go that far?' Dinamastre gave no answer. Laltu's mother cried for a few days. But since the village boys continued to bring the news that Yuvaraj was still searching for Laltu, hiding the bone of a cow in the pocket of his trousers, Laltu's mother consoled herself that even though her son was far away he would be safe there.

Danamuda Ashram School was 20 kilometres from Maricha-padar. The entire stretch of the road to the school was covered with forest. During monsoons the road became so muddy that it was impossible to ride a bicycle on it. So there was no alternative but to walk the entire distance. One morning Laltu, putting aside his vanity, set out from his home along with Dinamastre. His mother stayed at home, wiping her tears. Laltu's eyes were also brimming. But he was not crying. His heart had become somewhat stronger due to pain and egotism. He thought, *If my father and mother want me to go I must go. Let me die there....*

After Dinamastre left him in the school hostel Laltu opened his tin box. Inside the box he found a thin quilt made of rags to spread on the bed, a small bedsheet, a plastic bag of puffed rice, a few arisha cakes, a bottle of *kusum* oil, a cake of Lifebuoy soap, and another of Sunlight washing powder. These things reminded him of his mother's face and he felt like crying. He thought, *If I were to die now my parents will learn a good lesson!*

Danamuda Ashram School seemed like a jail to Laltu. You had to wake up and go to sleep at the sound of a bell. You had to pray, go to class, and work in the fields at the sound of a bell. Again at the sound of a bell you had to stand in a queue holding your plate and bowl like a beggar. *Chhe!* And the food! What was given in the name of rice was partly insects and partly bits of stone and the *dalma* was nothing but yellowish water.

Laltu remembered his parents. He remembered Manjula. He remembered his village pond, the water lilies in the pond, and the oleander flowers that bloomed at the Thakurani Gudi. He remembered the village dogs, the trees, and the stone of the Legrelega stream from where they used to jump into the water. He remembered his friends with whom he played kho-kho, kabaddi, and *bahuchori*. He remembered the newborn calf of their spotted cow. He was always close to tears and thought, *If I die now, my parents will learn a proper lesson!*

On his fifth day at school, while eating his dinner, Laltu found moringa leaves in the dalma. The salty, yellowish water in the name of dalma had almost killed his appetite in the last five days. Seeing the moringa leaves made him happy. Unlike other days he finished all his dalma without wasting it.

At night when he was sleeping along with the other boys his stomach started aching; he felt like relieving himself. He called the boy who was sleeping beside him once or twice but the boy did not respond. He tried to control his bowels by pressing his stomach. But he felt that it was just going to burst. It was pitch dark outside and he was afraid of going out alone. But after sometime he could not control himself. He got up and ran outside. He had not reached the verandah when watery stools burst and stained his pants and legs. When he started running the stools scattered all over the verandah.

What could Laltu do now? He kept running in one direction. He did not know when he left his school behind. He did not know when he reached the road that would lead him to his village. He did not know where he was going but trotted hurriedly towards the village. The sun had not risen yet. It was dark everywhere. In that darkness fireflies were fluttering. Frogs were croaking, *arr … awyen, arr … awyen*. But he was not at all afraid. Instead he felt like crying but controlled himself.

It was almost dawn when he reached Malgaon. Laltu washed his pants in the water of a crop field along the roadside, then washed himself and resumed walking in the same wet clothes. After crossing Malgaon he entered the forest. At that moment visibility improved with the coming of daylight. Laltu saw someone standing under a sal tree. He instantly recognized

Kartik Pota who had been admitted to his class three days ago. Seeing Kartik he was relieved. Kartik told Laltu that he had secretly left the hostel the previous evening as he was homesick. At night he had slept on someone's verandah in Malgoan. Before dawn he had got up and reached here. He was afraid of going through the jungle alone and had been waiting, hoping that if someone came along he would follow him to cross the jungle.

Laltu and Kartik walked ahead together on the jungle road. Though it was already morning an overcast sky made the jungle dark. When they reached a mahua tree two furlongs from the river Bori they heard a rustling sound. They stopped at once and tried to discern what it was. Just five to six steps ahead of them they saw a black animal inside the bushes. 'Bear!' shouted Kartik in fear and clung to Laltu. Laltu was so afraid that he did not even hear his shout clearly. Clasping each other they trembled. They had no energy to run away and shut their eyes in fear.

Suddenly, startled by the sound of barking, they opened their eyes. A black dog was before them barking continuously *bhow ... bhow ... bhow* as if asking *Who are you? Who are you?* Only then did life return to them. They smiled at each other. Their friendship began on that day. Nine years since then and nothing had disturbed that friendship. People say theirs was a watertight friendship, even though they were from different castes—one a Dom and the other a Gond—they ate off the same plate. However this was not so in Kartik's house but at Laltu's place. When they ate at Kartik's house they used separate plates. But they slept in the same bed to which Kartik's mother did not object.

◆

By the time Laltu reached Thutibor along with Rame Jagat and Dhania, Manabodo Sori had already gone to give the message to Baya leaving the tractor there. The other two men who had come along in the tractor sat on a stone under a tamarind tree and smoked *pika*. Fear was palpable on the faces of some committee members and others were expecting trouble. The moment Kartik saw Laltu he asked, 'What should we do?'

'What do you mean?' Laltu asked as if the question Kartik asked had no relevance.

'They say that we should let the tractor go,' said Kartik.

'If you wanted to release the tractor why did you seize it?' There was a tinge of irritation in Laltu's voice.

'We are not saying....' Kshirasindhu's sentence remained incomplete.

'Then who is saying?' Laltu exploded angrily at everyone.

'Then shall we go to jail?' It was not just Minaketan's question. Rather it was a warning for everyone.

'Have you stolen something that you need to go jail for?' Laltu asked.

'Don't you know Baya? Saala Habildar, Thanababu, all of them are in his grip. Don't you remember the jail you once went to...?'

'When I went to jail did I lose my moustache? Rather both my beard and moustache started growing there, isn't it?' Laltu smiled, interrupting Minaketan.

Minaketan laughed loudly at Laltu's humour, and so did the others.

The news of Laltu's going to jail had caused a commotion not only in Beheda and Dharamgarh region but also in the entire Kalahandi district. His name and photo were on the first page of the newspaper. In solidarity many known and unknown people had visited him in jail but Dinamastre had not gone even once. If anyone enquired about Laltu, Dinamastre replied sadly, 'For the last seven generations no one from our family has reached even the doorstep of a jail. But this boy has painted our faces black. Let him die in jail.'

On that occasion Laltu stayed in jail for thirteen days. He was not supposed to stay there for that long. But the police deliberately plotted to keep him in jail for at least ten days so that the news of his jailing spread around. The police had arrested him just two days before Dussehra when the court was on vacation. Therefore, Laltu could not get any legal assistance for his immediate release. Actually Laltu had beaten Paramanand Bag, the BDO, or the Block Development Officer, of Dharamgarh block, fifteen days before Dussehra, and the BDO, it seems, had filed a case against him the same day. But neither did the police come to arrest him nor did the constable enquire about the case.

Nine days before his arrest when Laltu was having dinner with his parents he heard his father telling his mother, 'Tell Laltu to go to the BDO and ask for forgiveness. If he accepts his mistake the BDO will withdraw the case. He has sent a message.'

Laltu did not respond and, as if he had not heard his father at all, addressed his mother, 'Give me some dal.'

A few minutes later Dinamastre tried again, 'The BDO is such a high-ranking officer but is showing pity because he is from our community. Otherwise by now Laltu would have been in jail. He would not be sitting here, eating comfortably.'

'Community's *b-o-y*!' Laltu exploded. He left his dinner unfinished and retorted as he rose, 'Saala, he is taking pity on me because he belongs to *our* community? And Chemeni

Aai...? Which caste does *she* belong to? Why did the saala eat away *her* pension money?'

'If you have to die for that old woman Chemeni, I have no problem. Go and die.' Dinamastre, equally offended, shot back.

Chemeni was an old widow from the same pada as Laltu. Three years ago her husband had died and a year ago her only son had left to work in the brick kilns of Andhra Pradesh. He neither sent her money nor did he ever pay her a visit back home. No one knew about his whereabouts or what he was doing. Chemeni's daughter-in-law was running the household on her daily wages. Chemeni's family included an eight-year-old granddaughter, a three-year-old grandson, and her daughter-in-law. Laltu had heard from the old woman that Nidhi Raut, the sarpanch of Beheda panchayat, had taken fifty rupees and a chicken from Chemeni to help her get an old-age pension. The old woman had requested Laltu several times to approach the sarpanch at least once and ask him when she would get her pension. Laltu had reassured the old woman but avoided doing the job. One day Rohit Majhi, the ward member of the village, brought news that the BDO himself would distribute pension the following day in the panchayat office. Chemeni, along with others, went to the panchayat office to collect hers. That day Laltu had gone to Beheda to buy kerosene. The old woman was coming back with her money when Laltu met her outside the panchayat office. Laltu asked her, 'How much money did you get, Aai?' The old woman was overwhelmed with joy and said, 'Son, I received three hundred rupees for five months.'

'Isn't the pension hundred rupees per month?'

'The Bido [BDO] sir deducted two hundred rupees for the paperwork.'

No one knows what happened to Laltu next but he went to the panchayat office immediately and learnt that the BDO had deducted two hundred rupees not just from Chemeni but from everyone. Laltu became furious.

'Why did you deduct two hundred rupees from these people?' he challenged the BDO.

'Who are you to ask this question? Are you my superior officer? Are you the collector?' The BDO sneered at him in contempt. Laltu could not control himself seeing the BDO's pride and contempt.

'Who am I? I am your father!' he retorted, slapping the BDO hard. If the sarpanch, ward members, and the others had not rushed immediately to hold him back Laltu would have slapped the BDO a few more times.

The policemen arrested Laltu fifteen days after this incident, just two days before Dussehra. The Habildar Negibabu of the Gotomunda police outpost took him on his motorcycle to Dharamgarh Police Station, saying that the BDO wanted to come to a compromise. But there was no compromise. So the police sent him to the court and the court sent him to jail.

It took another two days for the people of his village to find out that Laltu was in jail. When Dinamastre heard the news he felt low. He could not believe that his son would land up in jail one day. When people came to enquire about Laltu he said nothing. He only looked at the sky blankly.

'It is not a small thing to slap an official like the BDO! Laltu will be sentenced to at least ten years in jail. Let him face the music.' Nidhi Raut, the sarpanch, went about spreading such rumours. Two men from Palsapada village who had gone to sell their cattle in the Dharamgarh *goru haat* brought the news that the BDO had set the case in such a tricky way that no law-yers were available for Laltu's bail. Indeed no one from the vil-lage had even sought to bail out Laltu till then. However much Laltu's mother wept and pleaded, Dinamastre only repeated, 'As you sow, so you reap. He is getting whatever he deserves, let him have it. Let him stay a few more days in jail and learn a lesson.'

The person who released Laltu on bail was named Santosh Panda, an unknown person to the villagers. He was a corre-spondent and the district representative of a daily newspaper, the *Hastakshep*. He was not on good terms with Paramanand Bag, the Dharamgarh BDO. Once he had asked Paramanand for an advertisement of ten thousand rupees for the *Hastakshep*. Although he had agreed Paramanand evaded him every time he was approached for the payment. So Santosh Panda was look-ing for an opportunity to teach Paramanand a lesson.

No one knows where Santosh Panda got the news from but he came to the jail five days after Laltu's imprisonment. He enquired about everything, took Laltu's photo, and assured him that he would have him released on bail because he had not committed any robbery or murder. The next day the front page of the *Hastakshep* carried Laltu's photo with the headline: *Corrupt BDO Slapped, Young Social Activist in Jail.*

After that many people came to meet Laltu and everyone praised him. After thirteen days in jail, at last, Laltu got bail. There was another news headline in the *Hastakshep* two days after his release from jail and return to his village: *Corrupt BDO Suspended*. After this Laltu's importance rocketed in Beheda. Sarpanch Nidhi Raut no longer called him just 'Laltu' but 'Laltubabu'. The BDO returned the two hundred rupees which he owed to the elderly pensioners.

Laltu's identity as a social activist was established. The illiterate, the timid, and the poor started relying on him. He, too, did his best to involve himself in their sorrows and joys. His reputation grew. If someone's fever did not subside in three days Laltu would take him to the hospital on his bicycle. If someone's wall collapsed in the rain Laltu would go to the block office with an application. If someone was denied loan to buy a goat after seven visits to the bank Laltu would go to the bank and negotiate with the bank manager. If a married woman's limbs swelled and she needed blood after delivery Laltu would rush over and volunteer for blood donation without being asked.

One day Laltu had gone to visit Kartik behind whose house, near the *panishala*, were two papaya trees. One of them had two ripened papayas. In order to pluck those Kartik and Laltu were fixing a hook on a long bamboo pole when suddenly they heard someone crying. It seemed to come from Gaudapada's house. Kartik asked his mother if any elderly person in Gaudapada's family was ill. His mother was washing utensils at the panishala, so she stood up and strained her ears to hear what Kartik said but was not sure if something bad had happened to someone.

Leaving the hook Laltu and Kartik ran towards Gaudapada.

A crowd had gathered in front of Ghana Bagarti's hut. Ghana's wife was crying, beating her chest, and hitting her head. The women of the neighbourhood were also weeping. Watching them the children began to cry inconsolably. In the courtyard lay a corpse but it was impossible to identify it as Ghana Bagarti's. Nearly half of the face, and all of the left cheek, were missing. The blood clot on the wounds had darkened. Ghana had been dragged by a wild bear and his body was found by two of his companions after a vigorous two-hour search. Ghana worked as a temporary halia in Semi Marwadi's house at Beheda. That day before dawn he, along with two other halias, had gone to the Sahajkhol jungle to cut trees for timber.

'Is Semi Marwadi constructing a house?' Laltu asked Kartik absent-mindedly while returning from Gaudapada. The sight of Ghana's body had made him restless and uneasy.

'He already has a two-storeyed house and not enough people to live in it. So why should he build another house? Saala! In the name of mahua and neem seeds, he is carrying on a business, dealing in timber planks. He keeps sal, *dhawnra*, mahogany, and teak planks inside the truck and covers them up with sacks full of mahua, neem, and tamarind. Two trucks ply to Raipur every day.'

'Saala's plank business ends today,' Laltu said decisively.

By motivating young men from six neighbouring villages, the Sahajkhol Jungle Suraksha Committee was formed. There were twenty-eight of them between the ages of fifteen and twenty-five. Some of them were either in school or college, others were dropouts, and a few were illiterate. This committee made an announcement in the Beheda Sunday Market: *Except for fuel no one will be allowed to cut trees from the Sahajkhol jungle. A case will be filed against whoever is caught taking wood, and the wood will be seized.*

Though no case was filed against anyone within six weeks of this announcement, fifty to sixty loads of timber were seized. No one dared to try and get them released. They all lay in the backyard of Kartik's house. Laltu and Kartik went to the forester two or three times to talk about what to do with those planks, and about other issues relating to the forest. But they were unsuccessful. The forester who was in charge of the

Sahajkhol jungle had no official residence and was, therefore, staying in a rented house at Dahagaon. When the committee members went to meet him he was not there. Upon enquiry they learnt that a month ago he had disappeared from the village. Some villagers even complained that it was the forester who had allowed people to cut trees by taking bribes from them. When the committee members started seizing wood it put him in an awkward position because people who had bribed him asked him to return their money. To escape their wrath he began to hide in different places during the day and returned to his residence only at night. But how long could he evade people? Finally he left the village.

But one day, to everyone's great surprise, the forester reached Thutibor village and, parking his Rajdoot motorcycle under the tamarind tree near the crossroad, went straight to Kartik's house. At that time Laltu, Kartik, and a few others had gone to the pond. Kartik's mother was alone in the house. The forester did not know that Kartik's father had passed away the previous year. He shouted at Kartik's mother asking, 'Where is your husband? With whose permission has he piled up so much wood at his backyard? Call him. A case will be filed against his name.'

'What did you say, you shameless fellow? You will file a case against my husband?' Kartik's mother snapped back. 'You impotent, corrupt … thief yourself, *you* are calling *us* thieves! Don't you know who cut this timber? And you are shouting at us? Get out … I say, get out from here....'

Kartik's mother's rage frightened the forester. He realized that it was not the old woman speaking but Laltu from Marichapadar. He knew Laltu. He also knew that it was because of Laltu that the Dharamgarh BDO had been suspended. So he ran to the tamarind tree, jumped on his Rajdoot, and fled *ghutu* … *ghutu* as the engine spluttered and roared.

Returning from the pond Kartik and Laltu heard everything.

'What can be done now?' Kartik sounded anxious.

'This is the evil scheme of that saala, Baya. He has already started his foul play,' said Laltu thoughtfully.

'Then shall we release the tractor?' Kartik asked nervously.

'Release the tractor! Why? This time we will straighten him so well that the rogue will forget his father's name. Even if his God comes for it, never release the tractor. I will go to Bhawanipatna tomorrow. Somehow a case has to be filed.'

◆

That day in the afternoon when Laltu returned home from Thutibor he saw his father and Pangnia Budha from Firozpur seated on the verandah discussing something.

Pangnia Budha was the priest of Firozpur's Kalisundari Gudi. His body was as dark as ridge gourd seeds. His face was uneven and pockmarked. On the top of his left eyebrow was a tumour as big as a tendu. He was addicted to hemp. His eyes were as red as the *raktarani* flower. He drew a thick line of vermilion from the tip of his nose to the forehead. His greying tangled hair fell to his shoulders, and in it were three plaits with an oleander flower tucked into the longest one. On his shoulder, always, was an axe smeared with vermilion and oil.

Everyone, young or old, was afraid of Pangnia Budha. Children were afraid of his appearance and elders of his sorcery. Because he practised sorcery he was known as Pangnia the Sorcerer. Of course, to his face people called him Pujari Badu, Pujari Baba, Pujari Mamu, Pujari Aja, and so on.

Once, it was said, he had practised his black magic on Palsapada's Dama Jhankar. And what was the result? The moment Dama touched his food the rice turned to leeches and the gruel became blood. To others the plate was merely full of rice. But Dama saw leeches. While the others saw water or rice gruel Dama's eyes saw a bowl of fresh blood. Unable to eat or drink anything, within a fortnight, poor Dama wasted away and died.

On another occasion the old man was returning from Phupgaon from his in-laws' house. It was high summer and the scorching heat seemed like it would split one's head. Extremely thirsty, he went to a gauda's house in the next village and asked for a glass of buttermilk. There was curd in the house but the *gauduni* told the old man that they had no curd. Without uttering a word the old man flashed a smile and left. The next day in the morning when the gauda sat down to milk the cow, was it milk he drew? Only muddy water dripped into his pail. The gauda collected whatever curd and ghee they had and ran to the old man. Placing the hoard at Pangnia Budha's feet he paid obeisance to him by lying prostrate on the ground. The old man took a little curd and ghee in a small bowl, and dipping the toe of his left foot in it, said to the gauda, 'Drink it, saala'. The gauda, afraid for his life, drank it at once, closing his eyes. Only after that did milk flow from his cow again.

When he saw Laltu, Pangnia Budha stood up saying, 'Look, the boy has come', and showing his two rows of wheatish-coloured teeth said, 'I've been waiting for you for a prahara, son. Where have you been?' Without waiting for Laltu's reply he looked at Dinamastre and complimented him by saying, 'Mastre, your son has grown taller than you. Don't wait for too long to settle him.' Dinamastre did not say anything; he just smiled faintly. From his father's smile Laltu understood that there was some hidden purpose behind the old man's visit.

'Was there any work, Dadi?' he asked Pangania Budha.

Instead of a direct answer Pangania Budha looked at Dinamastre. His glance stated: *You tell him, Mastre. It will be nice if you tell your son.*

'It seems you have seized Baya's tractor?' asked Dinamastre.

'Why should I seize it? The committee members have seized it.' Laltu's voice was low.

'Who is the committee, son? Isn't it *you*?' Pangnia Budha emphasized.

'Won't you speak to them to release the tractor?' Dinamastre asked rather pleadingly.

'To live in water and to fight with the crocodile is regrettable. Son, you are still a child.' With a wicked smile Pangnia Budha continued, 'Baya is the all-in-all of our village and your father is a teacher in our village school. Try to understand this.'

Understanding Pangnia Budha's implications Laltu, as if ridiculing him, said, 'Why do you explain to me, Dadi? As an old man you should rather understand that without killing the crocodile it is not possible to build a house in water. You better go and tell Baya to do whatever he is capable of doing. Even at the cost of our lives we will not release either the timber or the tractor.'

And then Laltu walked straight into his house. Dinamastre and Pangnia Budha stood speechless.

Pangnia Budha had never thought that Laltu's answer would be as insulting as the retort he heard. That Laltu did not have even the slightest bit of respect for him made his blood boil. Furious, he shouted, 'Did you see that … did you see, Mastre! Not even a single drop of poison but your son like a *dhanda* snake is jumping at the tip of his tail. He will die soon, saala. As you sow, so you reap. Control him! Otherwise do not blame me later. I'm a pukka motherfucker. I don't even spare my father. Control him!'

During dinner Dinamastre tried to explain a lot of things to Laltu in many ways. The essence of what he said was that whatever social work his son was doing was not bad, but what was he gaining? What was his family getting out of it? Only loss after loss. His social activism was creating enemies all around unnecessarily. It was like eating at home but listening to abuses from others as if they were being fed by them. Never mind if he did not study. If Laltu did not work for the benefit of the family, at least he should not do things that would bring harm upon them. For the time being they had no difficulty for two meals a day. Let Laltu sit at home and eat comfortably. If he could spare some time for cultivation it would be good. He should not roam about like a ghost and listen to gossip.

Laltu sat silently, listening to everything like an obedient boy. He did not open his mouth though he wanted to say, 'Is this your idealism? While I was writing the seventh standard board examination, someone threw a piece of folded paper through the window and it fell near my feet. When I bent to pick it you were the one who scolded me. However much I tried to explain to you that I had never copied anything, you said angrily, "Being my son, Dinamastre's son, why did you touch that chit?" But today where is your idealism? Supporting Baya you are asking me to sit at home and eat comfortably. Why? Is it wrong to call a thief a thief? Is it a crime?'

But Laltu did not utter a word. He finished his dinner silently and went to the backyard to rinse his mouth. While returning he saw his mother sitting at the edge of the *chulha* against the wall, weeping.

'Why are you crying? What has happened?' he asked her. Continuing to sob and wiping her nose she said, 'We got you after worshipping so many gods and goddesses. You better obey your father. Pangnia Budha can set even a tender banana stem on fire. I am very scared ...' she almost choked.

'Are you afraid of Baya's foot-licking dog that came here to bark?' smiled Laltu. 'Do you think I will die vomiting blood if he plays his black magic? Is this how clever you are? Don't be silly. Stand up. Go and eat something.'

◆

Four

Semi Seth

◄◇►

Another truck drove up to Danteswaree Rice Mill. Semi Seth was boiling with anger and he rose suddenly from the wooden bed on the verandah of the mill. He leapt to his feet, his head started reeling, and everything went dark. He was about to fall but somehow managed to stay erect by holding the wall. 'Saale, they are shitting on the very leaf plates they eat off,' he muttered. Holding the wall, he shouted, 'Lakhan … hey Lakhan … are you alive or dead? Where are you? Missing for so long? Saala, you need ten hours to prepare a cup of tea?'

'Bringing now … Master….' Lakhan's voice came from inside.

Lakhan, Semi Seth's halia, had been with him for nearly twenty years. When he was a child of eight or nine, both his parents had passed away on the same night. Semi Seth had brought the orphaned child with him and given him a home. He initially guarded Seth's cattle. But when he grew older he moved to farming. For the last three or four years he was always by Seth to do his bidding. It was Seth who had arranged his wedding five years ago. He had no children. His wife did all the household work in Seth's house. All in all, Seth was Lakhan's father, mother, lord ... everything.

Lakhan came in carrying a cup of tea.

Standing against the cement pillar of the verandah with his face down, Semi Seth was thinking of something when he heard Lakhan's voice, 'Take this, Master....' Startled, Semi Seth raised his face and looked at Lakhan with drooping eyelids.

Lakhan saw that Seth's eyes had sunk deep into their sockets. Perhaps he had not slept for some days. His face had lost its usual glow. He looked like the withered flowers in bundled hair. Lakhan felt as if Semi Seth had not recognized him. His sight was dull and sickly like the moon under hazy clouds.

Handing over the cup Lakhan said reassuringly, 'Why do you worry so much, Master? Let a few days pass. You will see that every saala will come and fall at your feet saying, "O Sir", "Oh God". If they do not come to your door I swear that the rat snake will settle in their bellies.'

It was evident from Semi Seth's face that Lakhan's words did not reach him. Or even if they did he was unable to understand what Lakhan was saying. Touching his lips to the teacup indifferently he asked, 'Laba has not returned yet?'

Lakhan did not reply. He knew that however much Laba might try he would not be able to persuade the people this time. He was thinking about how to offer Seth some consolation. Poor Seth! Till the previous day if he asked someone to do some work, the person ran instantly to complete it. Look at him today!

In the morning Lakhan had met Mukun from Phalsapada by the river bank. Having turned a leader just a few days ago he said that the night before they had held a meeting at Ghana Jhankar's threshing floor in Jaitpur, where everyone had taken an oath on Goddess Danteswaree saying, 'If I go to work in Marwadi's mill for fifteen rupees a day, I'll eat my children's heads. I'll die instantly. My wife will break her bangles and become a widow.' Lakhan knew that Laba was an expert in deceiving people. But having heard these things from Mukun he knew that Laba's tricks would not work anymore.

Placing his half-finished tea on a plank Semi Seth asked, 'When did Laba go?'

'He left at the crack of dawn, Master. Must be on his way back,' replied Lakhan.

Seated on the bed Semi Seth muttered as if speaking to himself, 'I'll never let Laltu, that Dom boy, go. That motherfucker is the leader of this drama and has been after me for the last five years. If I do not push a dhawnra twig into his anus I am not Pawan Agrawal's son....'

◆

'As the rat snake swallowed the frog, Pawana swallowed the country'—the Pawana of this proverb, which is still in vogue in the Beheda region, is Pawana Seth, meaning Semi Seth's father Pawan Agrawal. He had another popular name, Dhol Marwadi. His belly, it seems, looked like a dhol, so behind his back people often called him by that name for fun.

In 1938 when Durjan Majhi was the gauntia of Beheda, Pawana Seth had visited for the first time, arriving in a bullock cart from Junagarh to Beheda haat to sell salt, kerosene, and other things. By then a resident of Junagarh for nearly twenty years, he had also built a pukka house for himself. Some twenty years before that Pawana Seth's father, Omprakash Agrawal, had moved with his family and children from Ratangarh in Rajasthan to settle in Junagarh, in Kalahandi district.

Beheda haat was held once in a week on Sundays during which clothes, oil, spices, salt, and kerosene were bought and sold. Since there was not much circulation of cash people bought what they needed in exchange of paddy, green gram, black gram, red gram, horse gram, sesame seed, linseed, and the like. A bullock cart took a whole day and night to reach Beheda from Junagarh. Loading salt and kerosene in the cart Pawana Seth would start his journey at dawn on Saturday from Junagarh and reach Beheda on Sunday morning.

Pawana Seth, aged about twenty, after coming to Beheda haat twice or thrice, met Durjan Majhi, the then gauntia of Beheda. Durjan was a Bhatra by caste. He was a straight-forward and simple man. Once when he had an ear ache many physicians and exorcists treated him unsuccessfully. The moment Pawana Seth came to know about his illness he ran to the gauntia's house asking his halia to guard his shop in the haat. He plucked a few leaves from a certain tree, crushed them in his palm, chanted some mantras, and extracting a few drops of liquid poured it into Durjan Gauntia's ear. At that time the gauntia was asleep on his left side with his right ear up. Pawana Seth put three or four drops of liquid in the gauntia's right ear and put his palm below the left ear. After sometime three or four live worms fell into his palm from the gauntia's left ear. Pawana Seth showed the squiggly worms on his palm to the gauntia and said, 'Had I been late by a few more days they would have entered your head and eaten up your brain!'

After this episode the gauntia recovered completely. A friend in need is a friend indeed. After that incident Pawana Seth became a true friend of Durjan Gauntia. Once, on the day of the haat, the gauntia called Pawana Seth to his house and said, 'Seth, why do you trouble yourself week after week? Let me transfer a plot of land to you. I'll be happy if you settle here permanently.'

The plot was located in front of the gauntia's house where Pawana Seth built a hut of dried twigs and mud and started his business. Within just ten years a large pukka house replaced the hut. It took only twenty-five years for that pukka house to become a two-storeyed building. It was not just a two-storeyed building; you could say it was a small palace!

The gauntia had gifted Pawana Seth only a piece of land to build a home. But within thirty years Pawana Seth had bought forty-five acres of fertile agricultural land from Durjan Gauntia, and after him, from his sons Sugriba and Biranchi. Was trade in kerosene, salt, and clothes so profitable? Impossible! People say that Pawana Seth, while digging for the foundation of his pukka house, found a large vessel of gold coins. By the time Pawana Seth died one-third of the Beheda village land was in his possession.

Compared to all the wealth, name, and fame that Pawana Seth earned in so short a time, the property his son Semi Seth collected was nothing. People even say that the son struggled just to take care of the property his father had accumulated.

◆

Whether others knew it or not, Semi Seth knew very well that the story of the golden vessel was a lie. He also knew that his father was a genius who could cultivate ragi in a field full of stones and earn gold—a skill he had acquired from his father. Otherwise after his father's death was it easy to have acquired seven trucks, three shops—a ration shop, a cloth shop, and another medicine shop—*and* a big rice mill? If he wanted he could buy not just Beheda but the entire panchayat. He was so powerful but Laltu, that useless Dom boy, was unnecessarily interfering in all his work and his plans.

It had been almost certain that Semi Seth would stand for the post of the sarpanch in the previous panchayat election. Had he contested he would have won easily. How much would it have cost? Just a few hundred thousand rupees. He was ready to spend that much and had already talked to Baya six months ago and finalized it. After closely studying the situation and calculating the votes from different communities Baya had revived the shakhas in three villages. Semi Seth also visited each shakha every three or four days along with Baya. Spending forty-five thousand rupees from his own pocket he had also organized *Asta prahari nama yagyan* in Jaitpur and a prayer sacrifice called the *Gayatri Yagyan* in Thutibor. The environment was so supportive of him that when the chariot moved around villages announcing the rebuilding of the Ram temple in Ayodhya, not only rich people, even those who had nothing to eat contributed a rupee or fifty paisa towards the bricks needed for reconstruction, shouting slogans in the name of Ram, ululating and chanting *Haribol*.

Everything was moving in the right direction. But at that very moment Laltu, the Dom boy, had punctured his hopes.

A fortnight before the election the Dom boy organized meetings in villages and said, 'Shall we worship the man who came flying like a dry leaf from somewhere but used his skills to turn into a stone? Shall we make him our king?'

'Correct! Correct! Yes, rightly said! No, we won't!' The illiterate crowds responded to Laltu's rhetoric.

The people's reactions shocked Baya. 'Why should we throw our money into water, Seth? Let's nominate your clerk, Laba. Holding the tail of the horse, you will be Krishna and he will be Arjuna. That Mahabharata will be interesting!'

But there was no Mahabharata at all.

That saala Dom boy along with his godforsaken friends nominated a Mahara boy named Raghu Meher as *their* candidate. Raghu had failed his undergraduate examination and had become a tuition master. They visited every village, every community, every household, and sitting on the edge of every hearth whispered, 'The person who is already someone's halia, can we make him our master? What a shame! *Chhi chhi!*'

Semi Seth had spent money like water, at least four hundred thousand rupees for Laba. In every village and community goats and sheep were butchered for a feast. He even made people take a vow in the name of Danteswaree. But can one ever believe these mean-minded people? Saale, after eating they wiped their hands on their heads. Laba Nial was defeated by two hundred and eleven votes.

However, the day Raghu Meher, with garlands around his neck, came triumphantly to the panchayat to occupy the sarpanch's chair, he was severely beaten on his back and buttocks. Semi Seth had bribed some village drunkard with two thousand rupees. The case was taken till the police station and the court. It is still going on. Raghu Meher's humiliation somehow consoled Semi Seth. But was it the gain he had sought to make up for such a huge loss?

Everything was due to that Dom boy's ploy. It was because of him that his plank business had been closed five years ago; because of him his godown of tamarind, neem, mahua, resin, and lac had been padlocked three years ago; and it was because of him that the family salt business had been ruined two years ago. Spending three million rupees, he had set up a rice mill but within six months the trouble started. Because of the Dom boy, for the last three days, the only work he did was swatting flies. People who once called him 'Master, oh Master' and were ready to even clean his soiled backside, now spoke impertinently to him because of the spell cast by that Dom saala. Their talk was now like an open slap.

Semi Seth continued his self-reflection. What had he not done for Marichapadar's Rainu, that beggar! Once after childbirth his wife's placenta could not be expelled. Whatever herbal medicines were tried, nothing happened. At midnight Rainu had hammered on his door. Clutching his feet he pleaded like a madman, 'Master, you are my mother and my father. Save me. Save my wife's life.' Semi Seth, without bargaining about the fare, asked his driver to fetch his commander jeep. Later Doctor Padhi of Dharamgarh had said, 'Your luck was strong. God saved her. Had there been an hour's delay....'

Rainu took seven months to reimburse the fare of the vehicle, giving Semi Seth five rupees one day, ten rupees another day, and so on. Had he, Semi Seth, taken even twenty-five paisa for the interest? His dharma did not allow him to take any. But what did he get for being so dharmic? Rainu's words to him yesterday were like a slap. 'If the government has fixed the rate for a day's work at twenty-five rupees, then we'll take only twenty-five rupees—not even a paisa less than that. The policy that we hold the horns while someone else drinks the milk will not work anymore. If anyone thinks that he is acting out of pity for us we don't need any pity. Let him mind his own business. Let him carry the sacks of rice on his back to load his truck. We have nothing to say.'

Semi Seth could hear the sound of a truck approaching. Altogether nine trucks were parked in front of the mill. What could be done? He was helpless! The mill had been closed for the last three days. Not a single worker was in sight. 'If the wage is not increased from fifteen to twenty-five rupees, we would rather die of hunger than come to work'—this is what the workers had clearly stated. Had it been for a rupee or two, Semi Seth would not have disagreed. But a ten-rupee hike! Impossible business! If their demand was met with, what was the guarantee that in future they would not ask him to dance at their whims? So he had decided never to yield. But a day's loss was at least fifteen thousand rupees. For how many days could he bear such a burden? He had to find a way out somehow.

At the sound of a bike Semi Seth raised his head. Before the bike stopped he got down from the verandah and strode up to reach Laba from whose expression he understood that he had not brought any hopeful news. He did not feel like asking Laba anything. Seated on the pillion of the bike he ordered, 'Go!'

'Where? Home?'

'No. To Baya.'

◆

Baya had probably heard everything already. Seeing Semi Seth he started saying, 'All this is because of that Dom boy's game, do you understand, Seth? If we do not control him now ... his mischief will grow by the day....'

Interrupting him Semi Seth said, his palms held prayerfully, 'That year, by mobilizing some wayward youths he seized your wood ... you, Sir, you did not punish him, you spared him, now you see how arrogant he has become? Now he is parading as a journalist. It is becoming impossible to even touch his tail anymore....'

'J-O-U-R-N-A-L-I-S-T! What a useless journalist he is!' said the mad lawyer mimicking him. 'By writing two lines, mixing some truth with falsehood from here and there, can one become a journalist? If so be a journalist to your family. Does that mean you will not obey your teachers and elders? Such pride! One day he came and asked me rudely, "It seems you want to change the name from Firozpur to Srirampur? Why?" What rubbish! Am I changing your father's name that I've to give you an explanation? It is up to us whether we name our village Srirampur or even Yamapur. Who are you, bastard, to poke your nose in it?'

'Last year ... no, no, the year before last,' Semi Seth corrected Baya's mistake and continued, 'you must have seen how regularly he wrote against me in the newspaper. Whether I buy mahua or *kandul* or lac in exchange for salt, Dear Son, why does your arse burn? When I dispatch either rice or mahua to Raipur via Debhog, why does your body itch, ache, and sizzle? He had written ... and you must have read it, *The Government is Losing Hundreds of Thousands due to the Black Marketing of mahua.* If the government incurred a loss, it is a loss. Have I robbed my properties from your house? Are you the government's offal-eating dog to bark bhow-bhow? Or are you the government yourself?

'There is a saying, if the Dom has only a *mana* of paddy, he is a *mahajan!*' Wiping the dirt from his neck Baya said, 'Whatever you say, Seth, if the Doms have some food at home, they show off so much that you can't even imagine ... and if they are able to read even two letters of the alphabet, they think that they know the Vedas and Upanishads by heart. They are not staying in the places assigned to them by caste rules. Because of their mobility, today, they do not respect even Indra or Chandra. Till yesterday we watched you removing the carcasses of cattle and eating carrion. During weddings and ceremonies you beat the dhol and *nishan* and ate rice seated on dunghills; after eating you tied the leftover in the corner of your towel and took some home for your family and children. Today, because you have two paisas, or you can afford to have two meals, or you are able to read two letters, does it mean you have become Brahmins? Doesn't Kavi Surya say, "By smearing mud from the Mandakini, can the village pig become a cow?" A pig is always a pig; a cow is always a cow. Forget about seven rebirths, if a pig meditates through a hundred rebirths can it become a cow? In the Tretaya Yuga, someone called Sambuka from your community was beheaded because he wanted to become a Brahmin by meditating. It was Lord Ramachandra himself who separated Sambuka's head from his torso. Whatever you say, Seth, there was a kingdom called Ram Rajya where everyone lived guarding his self-respect....'

Continuing, Semi Seth said, 'Very true, Lawyer Sir. Look at that poor old man Gandhi. To drive the foreigners away he left his food and drink and wore only a loincloth. He wanted the foreigners to leave India and for Ram Rajya to return. Let everyone live guarding his self-respect. But did the clever Doms allow him to do this? They have no self-respect. So for just using that term "self-respect", they shot him dead....'

Baya grew a little agitated at Seth's lack of knowledge of history. After shaking his head for some time and smiling he said, 'The Doms did not shoot Gandhi. He was shot by ... leave it. No point of discussing it now. But whoever shot him ... they shot him for good. Today it is a sin to even take Gandhi's name. He was basically a servant of the Muslims, our enemies. Therefore, he was a real villain. Yes, of course, there was another cheat at that time. He was not just a cheat but the leader of all cheats called Ambedkar. Have you heard his name?

'Is he the same person who seems to have written our constitution? Are you talking about him, Lawyer Sir?' Semi Seth replied hesitantly.

'Oh, yes, that Ambedkar.' There was mockery in Baya's voice. 'Is it a constitution or a big zero? Do you know his caste? Mahar. Mahars in Maharashtra are like Doms and the Ghasis of our area. So whoever is a Dom is also a Mahar, understood? The same community has a different name in different region.'

'Is it so?' wondered Semi Seth. Disbelievingly he asked, 'Are you saying that the country is run on the laws made by a Dom?'

'The country is governed by those laws; that's why it has come to this state. Don't you see that the Doms and the Ghasis have become the sons-in-law of the government? That's why they are pissing on our heads. If they study, they get stipends; if they look for a job, they have quotas. But their days are numbered, Seth. Let our party come to power. You will see we'll throw that Mahar's constitution out on the dunghill. We'll bring such laws that your mill will never be locked up.'

Semi Seth became agitated the moment the mill was mentioned. He had come to Baya with such hope but Baya was telling him that only if *his* party came to power something could be done about the mill. Exactly like the saying Radha will dance only when we have sixty *mahana*s of ghee. Gazing at Baya's face Semi Seth sobbed impatiently. 'But, Sir, it is now three days; my heart breaks to look at the mill. All around me is darkness. You are my only hope. Do something. Otherwise I'm ruined.' Semi Seth broke down and wept uncontrollably.

'Have patience, Seth. Patience is the answer to all problems. Why are you impatient like ordinary people? Give me a day.

We have to throw the dice very carefully. Let me think.' Saying so Baya fell silent. After a while he said, 'Bibhisana Gauntia's youngest son—that drunkard—what is his name?'

'Shankar. Are you asking about *that* Shankar, Sir?' Semi Seth replied quickly.

'What's your relationship with him like?'

'It is good, Sir. After all he is the gauntia. It is another matter that due to ill fate he begs for a living. Otherwise the entire village is his property. Whenever he asks me for anything I give it without questions. But, Sir....' Semi Seth was unable to understand why Baya was asking about that drunkard.

'Send him here to meet me in the evening. Let me see what can be done.' Baya sounded as if he had a solution to the problem.

Semi Seth wanted very much to ask him about something but then Baya had already switched on the radio and was searching for a station. Seth knew that Baya preferred to be alone while listening to the radio. If someone disturbed him at that time he got irritated. Seth was afraid of irritating the lawyer. Semi Seth had heard from several people that a few years ago after listening to the radio Baya had raged saying, 'Day and night, saala, repeats the name of that widow.' He had flung the radio against the wall so violently that its parts lay scattered everywhere. It was the day that the Emergency was declared.

'This is All India Radio. The news is read by....' Baya's ears stood up like those of a vigilant rabbit. Even though his eyes were on Semi Seth he was not looking at him; he was listening to the radio.

Semi Seth bowed worshipfully and stood up to go.

◆

Five

Muna

—◇—

The Fifth Day of the Strike of the Rice-mill Workers
Beheda, 17/11: Demanding a higher wage, the strike of the local
Dantesware mill workers has reached the fifth day today.
While the owner of the mill, Somen Agrawal, has requested
the workers to call off their strike, the workers have strongly
stated that their strike will continue indefinitely till their
demand is met.
It is significant to mention here that....

After writing this Laltu stopped. Lying back in his chair he closed his eyes for a while. What more could be printed, he wondered.

Last night Laltu had had a long discussion with Kartik about the strike for which he had taken the responsibility to lead. Their friendship had not weakened over the years and Kartik often came to Laltu for advice.

Kartik told him that two days ago Semi Marwadi's accountant Laba Nial had met him at midnight with ten thousand rupees saying that Seth would give him another ten thousand if the strike were called off. Kartik had told him, 'Get rid of this destructive mind of yours, Laba. For how long will you continue to be a dog, licking the Marwadi's feet, wagging your tail, and whining *kunw, kunw*? Instead of eating somebody's chewed bones it is better to have one's own stale rice water. In that lies satisfaction as well as dignity. You better forget your plan to foil the strike by tempting us with money. Instead, if it is possible, join us. We'll welcome you with a garland.'

At Kartik's fierce glances and strong arguments, which went against Semi Marwadi's plan, Laba ran away like a dog with its tail between its legs.

Laltu considered writing, *It is known from reliable sources that some selfish people are trying hard to foil the strike.* But if he did Santosh Panda would ask, *Who are those selfish people, what kind of attempts are they making, how did you come to know the sources—give me all the details. You have to provide at least some proof. They may be helpful in future.*

But how did one give proof of Laba's offer of money? Would Kartik's words suffice? Since he knew Semi Seth very well and was aware of everything he did, Laltu believed that what Kartik had reported was true. But without proof how would the others believe his words? Some people might even doubt him and say with a wink, *How come he rejected ten thousand rupees! What a saint! He must be the Mahatma of Kali Yuga!*

Laltu realized that it was already past ten. Yesterday Santosh Panda had reminded him several times to somehow send the follow-up news before sunset. He had only an hour and a half to finish.

The bus, called *Savitri*, reached Beheda at noon. Laltu used to send the news through the bus driver. The bus reached Bhawanipatna around 5 p.m. After collecting the news from

the bus driver Santosh Panda sent it to the head office of the
Hastakshep at Rasulgarh in Bhubaneswar.

Within an hour and a half he had to finish the news somehow and get it across to Beheda. Gripping his pen Laltu leant
over the half-written sheet: *While the government has fixed
the wage of unskilled labourers at twenty-five rupees a day,
the workers of the Danteswaree Rice Mill, for the last six
months....'*

Hearing noises outside Laltu stopped writing, and when he
concentrated again he realized that they were coming from his
verandah. Then someone called out his name! Dropping his
pen he rushed out.

Eight to ten women of his pada were surrounding someone
on the verandah. The situation was tense with the buzz of pain,
fear, and anger. Asking repeatedly what had transpired, Laltu
reached the group. He saw Muna from Beheda's Dompada, who
had a tailoring shop at Beheda's Sashtri Chowk, drenched in
blood. His white shirt had turned red. His eyelids, lips, and
cheek were so swollen that it was difficult to recognize him.

Muna started crying as soon as he saw Laltu. 'They beat me
mercilessly, Laltuda, by chasing....'

'Arre! *Who* beat you? And why?' Laltu asked perplexed.

'They were shouting they would kill everyone ... they would
also have killed me ... they torched my shop, Laltuda ... I'm
ruined....' Muna was crying inconsolably.

'Arre! Who were *they*? What happened? Why did they beat
you?' Laltu could not understand what had happened. Why
did someone beat the meek and gentle Muna? When his father
passed away two years ago Muna left school and started managing the 'shop', a small cabin made of wood and tin, located at
Beheda's Sashtri Chowk. This cabin housed a sewing machine.

Muna's father had brought the machine two years ago from Raipur. For ten years he had been pulling a rickshaw in Raipur. When his health deteriorated he returned to his village and set up the cabin at Sashtri Chowk. He began mending torn clothes and somehow managed his household. After his father's death, even though he was far too young to assume the responsibility, Muna managed the shop and took care of his mother and two younger brothers. Laltu could not believe that Muna could have any enemies.

When Laltu sat down with Muna on the verandah he saw that the back of his shirt was torn. Then he saw the weals caused by lashes which had turned blue. Perhaps he had been severely beaten with a stick. Blood had clotted where the skin on the back of his head had been split.

'Muna, my brother, please stop crying. *Who* beat you ... tell me ... *why*?' Laltu was getting impatient.

After some time Muna's weeping became less intense. He sobbed, 'In the morning I was stitching in my shop. A group of people from the village came at once ... Kame from Telipada. Gobinda and Jayaram from Ranapada. Tirlochan, Buti, Chandu, and Karuna from Gaudpada. Hari, Bidu, and Dama from Bhatrapada. Murli and Debria from Gondpada. Dhable and Naran ... some thirty to forty people. They had sticks, poleaxes, and small axes. Seeing them I was confused. I thought they were looking for Deba and Kurpa....'

'Deba and Kurpa? Who are they?'

'Don't you know them? They are from our pada....'

'Yes ... yes. Why were they searching for them?'

'Last evening, it seems, they had beaten Bibhishan Gauntia's youngest son Shankar....'

'Why did they assault him?'

'Yesterday being Monday, Deba's sister Urkuli and Kurpa's aunt Pheda had gone to the Mahadev temple but the priest refused to let them enter.'

'He *refused*! But why?'

'He said that Doms are not allowed to enter the temple.'

'Strange! But they do! My mother goes there regularly.'

'They used to earlier, but the priest said that Shankar Gauntia had asked him to restrict their entry from today.'

'Shankar said that? Who is he to restrict the entry?'

'It was to appeal against that that Deba and Kurpa had gone to Shankar last evening.'

'Then?'

'Their fault was that they asked him courteously! He was drunk. You know that the sun might rise in the west but he will not stop drinking even for a single day! While they were asking him, it seems, he roared, "Motherfucker Doms, have you learnt some lessons from your studies or are you zeros? Don't you know it is inscribed in the shastras that people from your community are not allowed to enter temples?"'

'What happened after that?'

'"Show us in which shastra it has been written," they asked him mildly. He then became uncontrollable. "Saala, you are speaking like this to me? You have the temerity to speak like this! Motherfucker Doms ... sisterfucker Doms ... carrion eaters ... have you forgotten your status? Next time if any horse-fucking Dom woman even steps inside the temple gate I'll force a crowbar into her ... and pour salt and chilli into it...."'

'Who will tolerate all such curses for his mother and sister? By drinking every day he has already ruined his health ... and you know Kurpa, how strong he is, he is a bodybuilder ... he gave Shankar a single punch and he fell to the ground ... then they ran away thinking that he was dead. But later they learnt that he was alive....'

'All this happened and I didn't know!'

'The mob came and threatened me saying, "Is this your father's property that you have set up a cabin here, you mother-fucker Dom? Get out, you motherfucker ... beat this saala ... cut this sisterfucker into pieces...." Yelling, they dragged me out from the shop ... beat me black and blue with their fists, kicks, and sticks....' Muna choked. 'They would have slaugh-tered me Laltuda ... to save my life I ran towards our pada ... I saw another group of people going towards our pada with sticks, poleaxes, small axes ... from there I ran towards your village....' Muna began bawling, 'They set fire to my shop ... they must have killed the people of our pada ... *L-a-l-t-u-d-a*....'

Laltu's eyes were already wet. In the meantime many people from his pada had gathered in the verandah. There was pain, anger, and fear on every face. Laltu wiped his tears.

Arranging to send Muna to Dharamgarh Hospital, he mounted a bicycle and set out for Beheda.

◆

Six

Mastrani

———◇———

A few hours to sunset but Laltu had not returned.

Placing a vessel on the fire to prepare dal, Mastrani once again went to the verandah from where she could see a long way on to the road. Far away near the *dalabat*, the crossroads of the village, where women go to smear oil and turmeric paste on dead bodies, she saw someone approaching. But, no, Laltu had left on a bicycle. Sighing deeply Mastrani turned and went inside.

What has happened to my child? Has he been harmed in any way? He had eaten only a palmful of puffed rice before he left. Where did he spend the day? Why has he not come back? The bookshop he had set up at Shastri Chowk of Beheda with a loan from the bank had been set on fire. This news had disturbed Mastrani deeply. Within a few hours she had already stepped up on to the verandah at least twenty times to glance towards the road and fifty times she had pressed her palms together invoking the goddess to fulfill her wishes: *O, Mother, Thuti Maili, let my son come back home unharmed. I'll offer you a young grey goat in the coming Diyal Jatra. Let no harm befall my son....*

It was already dusk but there was no sign of Laltu. Mastrani's mind was heavy. She was utterly frightened and overcome by some unknown dread. Dinamastre was also away from home. He had gone to Bhubaneswar or somewhere to see to his pension papers saying that he would come back in a day. But it was already three days and there was no news of him. What would she do now? Mastrani was about to cry but she did not because it was believed that weeping from fear was inauspicious.

'Are you home, Kaki?'

'Who is it?' Mastrani was startled and spat on her chest three times to ward off any evil spirits. It was already dark. Unable to recognize the person standing outside she once again asked, 'Who is it?'

'It's me, Kaki, Veeru. Have you not lit the lantern yet? Why are you sitting in the dark?' Veeru entered the house. He was the second son of Balu *mahuria* from the same pada. Almost a year ago he had left the music troupe and become a trader in cattle.

'Laltuda told me it would be midnight by the time he returns.'

'Laltu...? Did you see him?' Mastrani asked him impatiently.

'I went to Dharamgarh to sell cattle. While returning I met him near the police station.'

'Near the police station? Why?' Mastrani asked in a frightened voice. The scene of Laltu going to jail that year flashed in her mind. Agitated, she asked again, 'Why has he gone to the police station? What has happened?'

'Haven't you heard about the fight in Beheda village, Kaki?' Veeru continued, 'The upper castes united and mercilessly beat up the people of the Dompada. They've broken the heads of Bishia, Muna, Dhanu, and Madhu. Deba's and Ranka's legs are smashed.

And people say that it is doubtful whether Kurpa will live at all. All of them have been admitted to Dharamgarh Hospital.'

'Laltu ... has something happened to Laltu?' Mastrani asked fearfully.

'Laltuda? ... Nothing has happened to him. He has taken all of them and gone to the police station to file a case. Because the police inspector was not there—it seems he had gone to Bhawanipatna police station—he had phoned the officer to come back. After the inspector returns he will discuss the matter with him and come back home. That is what Laltuda told me.'

Mastrani was relieved to hear that nothing had happened to Laltu. Whatever the matter Thuti Maili Ma had heard her prayer. But why did that mad boy go to the police station to invite trouble? Let those who began the fights solve their problems. What was the need to meddle in it?

Mastrani was getting angry with Laltu. But when she remembered Muna's bloodstained, helpless face and his inconsolable sobbing, her anger disappeared. How cruelly those wicked men had hammered that innocent, orphaned boy. His face, eyes, and lips were so swollen that he was unable to speak clearly. The bruises on his calves and his back had turned purple. What would the condition of the others be? Will dharma forgive those wicked attackers?

After lighting the lantern Mastrani asked, 'What were you saying about Kurpa?' Three days ago Kurpa had come to their house to meet Laltu and because Laltu was not at home he had talked for hours. Even though he was smart he was a little foolish and grinned all the time.

'I don't know, Kaki,' replied Veeru. 'Laltuda was telling me that Kurpa has a head injury and that he is unconscious. It seems he had beaten Shankar Gauntia the day before. People were saying that it was because of Kurpa that there was such a big Mahabharata.'

'Why should he leave without beating him?' Mastrani shouted suddenly. 'If someone abuses your mother and sister using obscene language, will you let him go without a beating? Who will excuse that? Which man? Why should he leave him? The things that Muna said this morning ... Shankar should have been torn into pieces.'

◆

After Veeru left Mastrani finished cooking and waited for Laltu to return. After learning that nothing had happened to him her anxiety had somewhat dissolved. Instead of Laltu it was Muna's innocent, bloodstained face and Kurpa's smile that flashed in her mind.

In the afternoon someone told her that the people of Beheda village had burnt down the houses of the Dompada. Whose houses? Mastrani had visited the Dompada many times. She had visited Kurpa's, Dhanu's, and Devaki's houses. Their huts were made of twigs and mud. They were all poor, managing on daily wages. Only at the house of the gana was there some financial security. This was because they had ten acres of land from the king towards *gana bhogra*. But the gana house never offered any help to other Dom families during the hour of need. Property and wealth set them apart from the people of the Dompada. The upper castes would never have burnt down the gana house.

Then whose houses were burnt? Muna's? If they had torched Muna's house where would poor Bishakha takes shelter with her two children? Muna had said in the morning that they had burnt down his shop; that a single sewing machine supported all three of them—the mother and the sons. Will dharma forgive those shameless demons? Had Muna ever harmed them? If Kurpa punched that drunkard Shankar once they should have punched Kurpa three to four times. But why should they burn houses?

Why had Kurpa beaten Shankar? Because that drunkard abused his mother and sister! Who was that drunkard to not allow the Doms into the temple? Was Mahadev his father's property? It seems that the drunkard had threatened Deba and Kurpa, 'If the Dom women step through the door of the temple just one more time....'

'Did the Dom women shit in your mouth that you were forced to use such obscene language with them? In which shastra has it been inscribed that the Doms are forbidden to enter the temple? That shastra must have been written by you or your forefathers, fourteen generations ago. The shameless fellow is showing us the shastra! Haven't we read the shastras? Just because Bada Thakura blamed Chandaluni, an outcaste, he had to wander from door to door with a begging bowl. Has this also not been mentioned in the shastra?

'Your grandfather—a saintly person, may he rest in heaven—had earned great wealth. But his elder son, your uncle Sugrib, did not allow the village girls and daughters-in-law to live in dignity. How can Dharma Debata tolerate those great sins? So he bit him in the form of a snake and killed him. It was not just his death, but the death of all sin in the village as well. And your father, Bibhishan, was he any less? Kill some, beat others, and leave the cattle free in someone's crop to destroy the ripened harvest—these were his bad habits! Is it easy to digest so much injustice? In his youth wine and ganja gradually took his life. You haven't learnt anything even after so many blows? You poor, unlucky thing! Now you are wandering around holding a begging bowl, licking anything and everything, and yet cannot wake up? The other day, for just five rupees, didn't I see how helplessly you begged in front of Semi Seth? And you are the one to say that the temple is forbidden for the Doms. It has been inscribed in the shastra! I spit on that shastra of yours!'

Mastrani actually spat. But the spit did not fall on the shastra. It just fell on the front wall. Mastrani came to her senses. Laltu had not returned yet. What time of the night was it that the entire village was engulfed in silence? Probably everyone was asleep. Somewhere, far away, the dogs were barking. Was it Laltu returning home?

Veeru had told her that the police inspector had gone to Bhawanipatna or somewhere. Had he come back? If he had not then could Laltu leave Muna and others there in that condition and return? Never! Laltu was not like other boys who would leave someone in danger and escape! If he saw any injustice or heard of somebody in danger he was unable to sit still. He jumped straight into action, never considering the dangers. He had always been that kind of boy, even in early childhood.

Dinamastre, his father, utterly disliked this tendency of his. Dispiritedly, he often said, 'The boy is working without a wage. How will he be successful in life? Who knows how he will start a family?' Father and son clashed on almost every issue. Sometimes they did not so much as even look at each other for weeks. If the son faced the east the father looked westward. At that time Mastrani had wept a lot. Supporting her son she quarrelled with her husband. An enraged Dinamastre would say, 'You have spoilt him by pampering him, and you will live to regret it.'

'We have no one except Laltu, our only son. He is the apple of my eye. I got him after much fasting and penance. I offered *bel* leaves in the Mahadev temple for hundred and eight weeks. How can I not love him? How can I keep a distance? Since you have not given birth to him you will never understand the mind and heart of a mother.'

◆

When Mastrani was reminded of the Mahadev temple, Bididhungia Purohit's face flashed before her. He was the priest of the Mahadev temple, an unworldly person, a poor Brahmin who begged for alms from door to door. He would stand at the door and call 'Om Har Har Mahadev' three times, and wait silently. If you gave him a handful of rice he would take it happily. Otherwise he would move to the next house shouting 'Om Har Har Mahadev'. He would never demand anything.

Yes, he had another strange habit. If you gave him a palmful of rice or mung dal, he would openly ask for fifty paisa. 'I will buy *bididhungia.*'

Those who had money gave him an anna or two. But most of the people in the area were either small farmers or daily-wage workers. Where would they get money from? Whether he got a few coins or not, the old man after getting alms would ask, 'Give me a fifty paisa coin. I will buy bididhungia.' So he was called Bididhungia Purohit, the tobacco priest. To this day Mastrani did not know his real name. She used to call the old man Purohit Baba.

One day that Bididhungia Purohit came to beg for alms at Mastrani's door. After Mastrani had given him a *gidha* of rice and char anna for bididhungia, the old man wanted to say something but hesitated. 'Do you want to say something, Purohit Baba?' Mastrani urged him. He thought for a while and said, 'Ma, for a few days now I've wanted to tell you something. I do not think you want for anything....' Mastrani thought that the old man intended to ask for some money but he said, 'People who have nothing are also happy. Why do you always look depressed? Whatever may be your agonies, try to do something ... come to the Mahadev temple from this Monday. If you offer bel leaves to Mahadev continuously for hundred and eight weeks, all your sufferings will end.'

By then Mastrani had been married for seven years. She had already suffered three miscarriages. She had lost hope even after worshipping several gods and goddesses like Thutimaili, Bhainro, and Budharaja. She immediately agreed to the old man's suggestion. And it was no wonder that she conceived within two months of completing a hundred and eight offerings. Laltu was the result of Mahadev's blessings and hence his name, Lalatendu. His grandmother, Mastrani's mother-in-law, could not pronounce the name properly, so she called him Lula. Mastrani argued with her, 'Have you not got any other name that you call my son Lula? Why should my son be *lula*? Let his enemies be lula and *lengeda*.' After consulting Dinamastre their son's pet name was fixed. Laltu.

Why did no one raise any objections to the Doms entering the temple then? Did the Doms really go to the Mahadev temple? Of course not. As far as Mastrani knew she was the only person from Marichapadar village who visited the Mahadev temple, and that too because Purohit Budha had suggested it. Otherwise would she have visited it? In fact nobody from her own pada and from her village liked the idea of her going to the Mahadev temple. People said all kinds of things behind her back, 'Are all the village deities dead that Dinamastre has been sending his wife to Beheda's Mahadev temple?'

'Being in service Dinamastre has become a babu. Is that why the village deities are not good enough for him now?'

'Will a Dom woman become a Brahmin or a Marwadi by going to the temple of the Brahmins and Marwadis? Look how she wears her saree by pleating it. She also wears a petticoat and a blouse. She marks her forehead with sindoor, puts kohl in her eyes ... wow, my Brahmin lady ... wow, my Marwadi lady ... looks like a real Ma Kalisundri....'

Mastrani was sharply aware that the village women were envious of the way she dressed. Except for her, none of the other village women wore either a petticoat or a blouse with saree at that time. Of course they were poor and therefore could not afford to buy them. But they also did not know that a married woman had to put sindoor on her forehead. How would they know? They were all illiterate. If they had read some *pothipurana*s they would have known it.

But Mastrani had studied up to the fifth standard in Jogibahal Primary School in her village. Therefore, she had no difficulty in reading the pothipurana or *bratakatha*. She had another advantage. Half the population in Jogibahal village were Brahmins. Watching the way in which Brahmin girls and married women dressed, behaved, kept fasts, and celebrated different occasions, Mastrani learnt a lot. So when she married Dinamastre the practice of celebrating *margasira manabasha*, *savitri brata*, *sudasa brata*, and other such rituals reached Marichapadar through her.

Marichapadar was basically a poor village. Upon waking, the other village women first completed the unfinished chores of the previous day and went out to work in the fields. When it was midday they took a bath and returned home. Those who did not go out to work completed their household chores, finished cooking, and then went to take a bath at midday. But Mastrani got up early in the morning, finished her bath, and never stepped inside the kitchen before burning incense sticks near the Lakshmi handi which was hung from a sling in the grain store.

Whether it was the house of a Mali, a Gaud, a Gond, or a Dom, none of them ever avoided meat. In fact there was a proverb in the village related to meat, *If available it is Pausapunei; if not it is Sankranti.* But in Mastrani's house no meat was cooked on Mondays and Thursdays.

Watching Mastrani's practises, either out of envy or contempt, the village women would laugh among themselves saying, 'Dinamastre's wife is meditating to become a Brahmin.' Even though they laughed at her within five years they started imitating her. Some of them started wearing blouses, some put sindoor on their foreheads, and some even started celebrating margasira manabasha. Some of them took a bath in the morning before going to the fields for work, and after finishing their work bathed again at midday before returning home.

Therefore, Mastrani was hardly bothered when there was gossip in the village about her visits to the Mahadev temple. She thought that all this talk arose from envy. A time would come when they would turn silent.

But she was proved wrong.

Once Majhi Baba, the priest of the village Thakurani Gudi, visited them in the evening and said to Dinamastre, 'I hear that our daughter is going to the Mahadev temple. Is that so?'

According to the village custom Majhi Baba was Dinamastre's uncle. So the old man addressed Mastrani as daughter.

'Yes, Mamu, she is,' replied Dinamastre anxiously.

'Why? Have all the gods and goddesses of the village died? They have been with us for ages, listening to our pleas and guarding the village day and night. Like parents they protected everyone from all sorts of danger and illness. If they were not here then you, me, even this village wouldn't be here. Is it that you don't believe in them that you send your wife to the Mahadev temple? Do you think that Mahadev is greater than our Thakurani? Is he greater than Budharaja, Bhainro, or Bhima? Is he more powerful than Thutimaili or Jalkamni, the seven sisters? Is this all the brains you have after studying so much? The more you study, the more foolish you have become. *Chhet....*' Majhi Baba continued levelling his charges in a voice full of anger, disgust, and disdain.

'Mamu, I never said that they were big or small. They are gods like Mahadev,' Dinamastre cut short Majhi Baba's arguments.

'I am not saying that Mahadev is not a god. I want to ask whether he is *our* god or the god of Brahmins and Marwadis?'

'Is god a piece of land or an ornament that we can say it isn't yours but ours, or it isn't ours but yours, Mamu? A god is a god for everybody.'

'You are teaching me a good lesson, Mastre. Had Mahadev been our god, would Dhol Marwadi have ever built a temple for him? Has he built a temple for Danteswaree? Has he built a temple for either Thutimaili or Thakurani? He hasn't. He built a temple for Mahadev; he also built a temple for Jagannath. But why didn't he build a temple for Thutimaili? Tell me, why?'

'Does Thutimaili live in a temple so that....'

Majhi Baba interrupted him, 'Yes ... now you are coming to the point. Thutimaili does not live in a temple, do you know why? Is it only Thutimaili? None of our gods and goddesses lives in a temple. We are only agricultural workers, labourers, and poor people. Our house is either a room or two. A hut made of mud and twigs. Then would our gods and goddesses like to live in big temples instead of living either under trees or in huts? We are their children and they are all our parents. When the children live in hunger will the parents eat *khiri* and *khichiri*? They are content with a little rice or a drop of *mahuli*. Anything more would mean either a chicken or a goat. Isn't that so? And for Jagannath, it seems, not less than *shathia pauti* will do for a day....'

'But, Mamu....'

'Listen again. Whether it is Mahadev or Jagannath they need regular worship and varieties of food as prasad every day. But we hardly worship our gods and goddesses once or twice a year. When we offer them whatever little we have on the occasion of Nuakhai, Pual Uwansh, or Chaitpuni, they are pleased and we, too, feel good throughout the year.'

After Majhi Baba's irrefutable arguments Dinamastre remained silent. While taking leave Majhi Baba said, 'It's for your well-being that I came to explain all these things to you, now it's up to you to decide. If the village gods and goddesses get angry with you or cause you any harm, you shouldn't blame me.'

Hidden behind the door Mastrani was listening to the conversation between Dinamastre and Majhi Baba. What he said was true! What if the village gods and goddesses got angry and did them some harm? Her heart pounded with some unknown fear. 'O Mother Thakurani, O Mother Thutimaili, O God Budharaja, Bhima ... we have never disobeyed you ... do not take offence for our misdeeds....' She muttered clasping her hands, head bowed.

After much thought she told Dinamastre at night, 'It is Majhi Baba who scared us. Why should our village deities do us any harm? Have we ever disobeyed them? I had three consecutive miscarriages but did we ever blame them? I took a vow in front of all of them that if I had a baby I would offer sacrifices.'

Mastrani's visits to the Mahadev temple did not stop. For years, if not every Monday, she surely visited the temple at least once or twice a month. After the death of Bididhungia Purohit his son Biswanath had been in charge of the temple for the last seven to eight years. He called Mastrani 'Kaki'. The interesting thing is that within a few years those who once criticized Mastrani's temple visits started going to the temple themselves. Now almost everyone in Marichapadar visited the Mahadev temple. Just last week Mastrani had met Pujari Baba's granddaughter-in-law in the temple. Had the old man been alive would he have allowed his granddaughter-in-law to offer worship there? Who knows?

◆

A burst of fierce barks of the dogs outside....

Had Laltu returned? Mastrani tried to listen. No, no sound of footsteps. The night was calm. It was on dark nights that the dogs barked anxiously seeing spirits and witches. It was the night after the full moon, an opportune time for witches and spirits to wander around. Would Laltu be walking home in the dead of night? No, he should not. It would be best if he did not. Three days ago Kishu Bodkia's youngest daughter-in-law of Malipada had died, unable to deliver her child. Sanu Majhi's son Phagnu was heard telling others that last night some people had seen her spirit on the bank of Legrelega stream, massaging her newborn infant. Laltu should not come. One must not ignore the existence of evil spirits and witches. You never know, anything could happen anytime.

But Laltu did not believe in evil spirits and witches. He simply laughed at *shirakaleshi*. That year when the *Chaitra Ghant* was going round the village in procession, he insulted and humiliated Phagnu's mother, who was usually possessed by Goddess Thutimaili. For days after that the poor woman did not dare show her face in the village. Shall we see what happened?

It was the scorching sun of Chaitra. Chaitra Ghant was going from house to house. As usual Phagnu's mother was possessed by Thutimaili. Her hair was dishevelled, a garland of red hibiscus flowers was around her neck, and she held a *trishul* smeared with sindoor. Tongue lolling and large eyes staring, Phagnu's mother was running ahead, shrieking. Following her were four virgin girls holding the ghant decorated with *palasa* flowers, the aged priest, and some villagers with musical instruments, all in a big procession.

Whenever the ghant reached somebody's door the women of the house came out to worship it by burning resin and placing turmeric-smeared rice on it, ululating all the while. In return Thutimaili, in this case Phagnu's mother, blessed them by blowing and puffing into their ears and putting the trishul on their heads.

Till then no one knew where Laltu was. But suddenly he came up at a run. Almost panting he asked, 'Where is Phagnu's mother?' From his urgency people thought some mishap had happened. At that moment Phagnu's mother was blessing Banabasa's daughter Kaikee by placing her hand on the girl's head and whooshing into her ear. Anxious, people repeatedly asked Laltu, 'What happened ... what happened?' Laltu, still panting, said loudly, 'Phagnu has been bitten by a cobra under the peepal tree....'

People ran towards the peepal tree anxiously.

'Oh, my dear son!' wailed Phagnu's mother and, throwing her trishul away, ran along with them. When they reached Phagnu they saw that he was drunk on mahuli and talking to a dog in Hindi. Whenever Phagnu asked the dog, *'Kya hua, kya hua?'* (What happened, what happened?), the dog answered, whimpering *Kyun ... kyun ... kyun.*

Everyone just laughed heartily.

That day it was proved that the possession of Phagnu's mother by Thutimaili was a lie. If she were possessed would she have run anxiously to save her son? Would she have heard Laltu at all?

'Only if there *is* a Thutimaili, will *She* possess her?' Laltu remarked laughingly. 'Just as Phagnu's mother getting possessed by Thutimaili is a lie the existence of Thutimaili is also a lie. Whether it is Maili or Thakurani—everything is pure nonsense.'

'Keep *q-u-i-e-t*! ... Do not blame the gods and goddesses ... *Tush*!' said Mastrani in a frightened voice.

Laltu laughed loudly and said, 'If your Thutimaili really exists, shall we see how she breaks my neck and kills me tonight?'

Mastrani shut her ears by thrusting her fingers in them. Her eyes were filled with tears. She said, 'Don't utter such ominous words, you mad boy....'

Laltu laughed loudly and ignored Mastrani's warnings.

Right from childhood he had always been obstinate. He would never compromise ... such a fiercely determined boy.

◆

Laltu at seven was in the second standard. Bididhungia Purohit was still alive. The old man once came begging for alms. Standing on the verandah he announced, 'Har Har Mahadev, Har Har Mahadev.' Mastrani came out from the kitchen and paid obeisance to the old man by lowering her head to the ground. Laltu was standing nearby. 'Pay obeisance to Baba, my dear child,' said Mastrani. Laltu shook his head and said 'No' and fixed his gaze on the old man.

'Good boys obey orders and respect elders,' Mastrani coaxed him in a sweet voice.

Laltu made a face by sticking out his tongue and said, 'Good boys do not obey. They do not respect elders....' He wanted to escape from there.

Mastrani quickly caught his hand. She forced him, 'Pay obeisance ... you are becoming too much....'

Laltu thrashed about on the verandah and shouted, 'I will never do obeisance ... never pay any respect to this old beggar....' He shrieked loudly and bit Mastrani's hand hard.

Unprepared for this Mastrani's face paled with humiliation.

'He is a child ... why are you forcing him, Ma? Leave him, let him go to play.' The old priest smiled and said. Had it been anyone else he would have cursed angrily. He was, above all, a decent man.

When she thought about the curse Mastrani was reminded about another incident.

Krupasindhu Baba was a follower of Mahima Dharma. He used to come to Jaitpur Tungudi once or twice a year, where he was certain to visit Dinamastre's house for alms. One day he reached the house in the morning, chanting *Sriguru saranam mahima swami alekh alekh*. Mastrani slipped puffed rice into black tea in a banana-leaf cup and gave it to him. Babaji was sipping tea, gently shaking the leaf cup. Laltu and a few other boys of the neighbourhood were staring curiously at him. When Babaji was drinking tea the ends of his long moustache kept dipping into it.

When Babaji finished his tea some tea-soaked puffed rice was left in the leaf cup. Krupasindhu Baba called Mastrani and said, 'Take this, Ma, and feed it to your son as prasad.'

Mastrani gave the leaf cup to Laltu and said, 'Eat it, dear.'

'*Yawks!* The old man's *singhan* has fallen here ... *thu*....' Saying so Laltu spat and flung the leaf cup away.

Krupasindhu Baba got up with a jerk and said angrily, 'Today I can clearly see the future of this child. He will be either a thief or a dacoit when he grows up. That is for sure.'

Babaji had not finished when Mastrani slapped Laltu hard across his cheek. Laltu did not cry even after such a blow. It was Mastrani who had wept the whole day and suffered.

About four years after that incident Laltu was in fifth or sixth standard in Jaitpur School where he had always stood first ever since he enrolled as a student.

It was Basant Panchami, a day to worship Goddess Saraswati. In the morning when Mastrani, after packing a coconut, incense sticks, flowers, and banana into Laltu's bag, searched for him, he was nowhere to be found. Mastrani thought he might have gone to pluck flowers along with his friends. On festive days children enjoyed doing such small tasks. Had he come sooner his father would have given him a lift on his bicycle and dropped him at the school on his way to his own school, which was also celebrating this puja. Not seeing Laltu anywhere Mastrani grew restless.

'I'm getting late, send him along with his friends.' Dina-mastre said and left for school. Mastrani went out in search of Laltu. All his friends were ready to go. Where had this naughty boy gone? Someone said, 'Laltu along with Tekaru from Soripada was catching fish in the ditches at Kurlumuda.'

Mastrani could not believe her ears. 'Oh, God!' she said and rushed towards Kurlumuda. The two boys were, in fact, busy baling out water, their bodies covered with mud. It was impossible to recognize them.

'Oh, God!' Mastrani's heart started beating faster. 'Both of you, what are you doing here on this auspicious day? Today is the day for worshipping Saraswati. Don't you remember? Let's go....'

'No ...' said Laltu in a firm voice.

'Why?' Mastrani was astonished.

'No ... nothing ... I will never go to school,' Laltu repeated in a firm voice.

'What has happened dear?' Mastrani entered the muddy water. She drew him to herself and asked, 'Did someone scold you?'

'Leave me ... set me down ... I'll not go ... set me down....' Latlu struggled hard.

However much Mastrani tried to explain, and even begged, he refused to listen to her saying, 'I'll not go to school, set me down, leave me.' Getting angry, Mastrani hit him on his back. Bringing him home, she threw him down on a cot. Tossing on the bed, Laltu continued crying.

'Cry, you black sheep from somewhere.' Saying this Mastrani entered the kitchen.

Sobbing, Laltu fell asleep.

After cooking got over, when Mastrani came out to wake Laltu for a bath, she felt that he was running a high temperature. 'What happened to my beloved? Why did I, a sinner, raise my hand against him?' Mastrani cried bitterly.

The next day when Dinamastre went to Jaitpur School he learnt that Laltu had not even deposited his contribution for the puja.

After few days when Mastrani cajoled him a lot Laltu then revealed all his secrets one by one.

A week ago on Saturday, after the games hour, a meeting was organized in the school for the Saraswati puja. The objective of the meeting was to discuss how much money to collect from each class and to decide the items for prasad: whether *chudaghasa*, *seo bundi*, or *puri* and *payas*. While discussing the contribution, Mishra Sir, the headmaster, announced that the student who contributed the most would be the host for the puja. A student from Telipada, Surath Sahu's son Brunda, raised his hand and said, 'I'll give ten rupees.'

'Good!' Headmaster Mishra Sir said. 'If anyone wants to give more than ten rupees, please raise your hand.'

'Fifteen rupees.' The boy who stood up was Lalatendu Duria, Dinamastre's son.

The children clapped hard.

'Even if you give twenty-five rupees instead of fifteen, you cannot be the host for the puja. Sit down,' Mishra Sir ridiculed him.

At that the children did not respond as they could not understand why Mishra Sir had said what he did. Everyone looked around. Puzzled, Laltu stared at Mishra Sir's face.

'Did you not understand why I said so? Arre, what is there not to understand? If we human beings do not touch water from the Doms how can Goddess Saraswati eat food offered by them?'

Except for ten to fifteen Dom boys the rest of the children laughed at Mishra Sir's reasoning.

'Arre, what is there to laugh? *We* are not saying this. This is inscribed in the shastras. Dear Lalatendu, your father is also a teacher. Go and ask him, during Saraswati or Ganesh puja does he touch the food that is offered to the deity? Never mind the others from your community,' Maharana Sir added.

Offended and angry Laltu was almost in tears. Discrimination against them prevailed in school as well. However thirsty they might be the Dom children could not touch the clay pitcher in which drinking water was stored. They quenched their thirst only when one of their upper-caste classmates poured water into a particular glass for them. Laltu was also obliged to do the same. Since it had become a habit he had never felt particularly humiliated. But today's insult was very painful. Anger and bitterness made him restless.

That day after returning from school Laltu hung his school bag on the nail adjacent to the photos of Lord Ganesh and Goddess Saraswati which he had pasted on the wall. He stood before them and cried bitterly. 'It seems you won't eat prasad from my hand. If so, eat my spit, eat my singhan!' He spat on the photos, and squeezing mucus from his nose smeared it on their smiling lips. He then tore the photos into pieces and threw them in the garbage.

Mastrani cried a lot that day. She was afraid that the wrath of Ganesh and Saraswati might befall her son and make him illiterate. Secretly she prayed, 'Oh God, please forgive my son. He is just a child. He has no sense at all. Do not mind his sin. Whatever punishment you want to give him, give it to me. Kindly forgive my ignorant child.'

That day Mastrani explained to Laltu lovingly by patting his head, 'Never behave with any god or goddess in that manner, my dear. Mishra Sir is wicked minded; that's why he said such a thing. It is not good for you to get angry with any god or goddess for whatever *he* said.'

Laltu, then a student of either fifth or sixth standard, argued, 'Ma, you are saying that Mishra Sir is wicked. Where did he get that wicked mind? Was it not Ganesh who gave him such a wicked mind? Both you and father tell me that Ganesh is the God of Knowledge. If it so it is better to break the neck of such a God of Knowledge.'

Sensing that her son's anger had not cooled Mastrani did not want to dwell on the topic. But afterwards she noticed that Laltu had completely lost faith in gods and goddesses. If there were any talks or rituals related to gods or goddesses he would ridicule them. Thereafter, Mastrani never forced him to participate in any rituals. If Laltu ridiculed her or was angry because she fasted for a puja Mastrani avoided him by saying, 'Go away, you mad boy.'

But today, after so many years, when Mastrani remembered Laltu's arguments on that far-off day, she felt that he was quite right. That God who sowed discrimination among people, seating one on his lap and throwing another far away, what kind of God was He?

She had been going to the Mahadev temple for so many years now but had she ever got a chance to pour water on the linga or offer flowers and bel leaves on her own? Whatever prevailed when Bididhungia Purohit was alive, the same thing continued during his son Biswanath's time. The moment Mastrani entered the temple Bishua, Biswanath's nickname, would say, 'Kaki, keep your puja tray there.' Placing her tray Mastrani sat down with folded hands and closed her eyes. It is Bishua who broke her coconut while chanting mantras, poured water, and offered flowers and leaves to the linga.

Mastrani has never heard Bishua saying the same thing to Semi Seth's fat wife! Rather she had noted that whenever that fat woman visited the temple, she broke her coconut, poured water on the linga, and offered flowers, leaves, and prasad to the deity. Bishua just stood, stared, and chanted his mantra.

So, did Mahadev believe that the overweight woman was a human being and that she, Mastrani, was not? She questioned herself. Was it because she was a Dom that Mahadev hated her? If that's not so why did He not take offerings from her personally? If He is the God of all castes and communities why did He not cut the tongues of either Shankar or Bishua with his trident when they drove away the Doms from the temple entrance?

If someone hated to touch you would he want to see you prosper? Can he? One who turns up his nose at you will he listen to you however much you pleaded with him during your time of need? Was the belief that she had got Laltu through Mahadev's blessings a lie?

Suddenly an inner voice within Mastrani answered, 'Yes, yes, it's a lie; it's a pure lie. Even such a belief is useless and complete nonsense!'

◆

Seven

Santosh Panda

———◦———

The phone rang when Santosh Panda was about to clean his tongue after brushing his teeth. Saala, in this profession, one did not have time even to die. Angrily he pressed the tongue cleaner a little harder on his tongue. Ouch! Whenever he took a few extra pegs at night his tongue felt sore the next morning. If he was not careful while cleaning his tongue there was a risk of injuring himself. He cut his tongue and blood oozed.

Santosh tasted salt, which meant his tongue had indeed been cut. Now he would have to suffer the entire day. Whatever he ate something it would burn and sting. *Tush!*

Santosh's wife Mitali rushed to him saying, 'SP'.

'Tell him I am in the toilet,' Santosh Panda said irritably and entered the washroom.

After his bath he stood before the mirror to comb his hair. Mitali brought some *chakuli*s and mint chutney to the dining table and said, 'The old fellow has already called twice.'

'Why didn't you tell him that I had gone to the bus stand?'

'But you told me to tell him that you were in the bathroom. And now you say....'

'Who is the old fellow you are talking about?' Santosh asked turning towards her.

'Don't be nervous. It is not the old fellow, your boss. It is the SP,' Mitali chuckled.

'Oh! ... Then why don't you say so ... I thought it was my boss. Saala, you are the publisher of a newspaper. You should worry about how to reach the top position in your business. Instead of doing that who gave you this bad advice to get into the cassette business? I am sure, Mita, after a few days the old man will tell us to sell lottery tickets. Saala, he is always running after money and....'

The 'old fellow' referred to was none other than Suranjan Mohanty, the editor and the owner of the *Hastakshep*. Abandoning a high-salaried job, he had got into the newspaper business fifteen years ago. He was extremely ambitious. His father had been an MLA for eighteen months, so his dream was to become a chief minister. His first step to fulfill that dream was the *Hastakshep*. The old fellow was not in any political party; he was independent. After gauging the political situation, perhaps, he would make his move. Apart from publishing the *Hastakshep* the old man had already produced three films in the last fifteen years. The interesting thing was that he himself wrote the dialogue and screenplay for these films. And all of them flopped.

So the old man was now after the cassette business. Forget about the profit Santosh was sure that even the capital money would not be returned. Since he was employed under him he had no other option but to agree with him chanting, 'Yes sir. Yes boss.'

The old man had rung up yesterday, 'All district representatives have been given responsibilities to distribute cassettes. Oversee them.' Three cartons packed with cassettes arrived from Bhubaneswar, and Santosh had had to run to the bus stand very early in the morning to collect them.

'Saala, it is becoming difficult even to collect money from the newspaper agents. Apart from this, one has to arrange for advertisements for the newspaper. And the monthly target is fifty thousand rupees. On top of it the latest order: to sell cassettes. Saala, when will he collect the news or write the news report? Instead of a news reporter it would have been better to have become an assistant to some contractor.' Santosh Panda spoke angrily to himself.

Dressed in jeans and T-shirt he came to the dining table. Absent-mindedly he took a bite from chakuli with some chutney and tried to swallow. It was painful because of his wounded tongue. Just then the phone started ringing. He indicated to Mitali to attend the phone. Picking up the phone Mitali said, 'Hello ... Yes Sir, I'm giving it to him.'

Santosh enquired with raised eyebrows, 'Who is it?'

'SP,' Mitali whispered.

'Saala, if he wants something he will ring continuously,' murmured Santosh.

S.P. Nakul Rath was actually a deputy superintendant of police (DSP) by designation. He had joined as a sub-inspector and had been promoted to DSP. Six months ago the superintendant of police (SP) had retired; thereafter, Nakul Rath had taken charge as the SP. The staff of the police department called him Pumu behind his back, meaning *puruna musha*.

The local MLA, Panchanan Suna, who was Santosh Panda's classmate in college and now the minister of tourism in the state government, was angry with Pumu for some reason. Pumu was afraid that Panchanan would pressurize the top officials and send out a young officer as SP. So Pumu had requested Santosh repeatedly saying, 'The minister is your friend. He has some wrong notions about me. Kindly recommend my name for the post.'

Santosh Panda held the receiver, 'Hello Sir … namaskar. Sir, the work has been done. It was already dark when I got back home yesterday and I thought you must have gone to sleep by then. That's why I didn't disturb you.'

'Oh, no, no, Santoshbabu … it's no disturbance at all. You can ring me any time you like. Yes, the minister sir just called me. I thought I should convey my thanks to you,' Pumu spoke gratefully.

Santosh knew Pumu's nature very well. Therefore, he also replied warmly, 'That was my duty, Sir. If I were in trouble, would *you* not have come to *my* help?'

'Santoshbabu, you haven't given me such a chance yet,' said Pumu as if it were a grievance. Before Santosh could reply he suddenly remembered something and continued, 'Oh … yes … do you have any reporter in Beheda for your newspaper? Someone named Chandrasekhar?'

'He is not Chandrasekhar, Sir … he is Lalatendu … Lalatendu Duria,' Santosh Panda corrected him.

'Yes, yes, Lalatendu Duria … yesterday a case was registered against him at Dharamgarh Police Station. Do you know that?'

'A case! Against Lalatendu? But why?'

'Do you know him well, Santoshbabu? Really well?'

'What are you asking, Sir? I personally requested the managing director to appoint him as a reporter. He is a very good boy....'

'Santoshbabu, because you are a simple and good human being everything looks good to you,' Pumu laughed. 'Do you know what he did yesterday?'

'What, Sir?'

'By instigating the Doms of Beheda village he has caused a Mahabharata.'

'Sir, this must be wrong information. From what I know of Lalatendu he is not at all like that. Besides, he rang me yesterday evening about the fight. He told me an entirely different story. It seems that the gauntia of the village did not allow the Doms to enter the temple; that's why there was a fight. The same person instigated and inflamed the villagers who attacked the Dompada. Many people have been injured. Many houses were burnt down. Lalatendu told me that people even torched the small bookshop he owned.'

'Have you already sent the news to be published, Santoshbabu?' Pumu asked worriedly.

'Sir, yesterday he rang me at six in the evening,' said Santosh. 'He gave no details. Only after Lalatendu comes today....'

'Whatever information you have is correct. Only the origin of the fight is not true. Your reporter has kept you in the dark. Yesterday my *samudi* rang me up and told me everything....'

'Who? Who did you say, Sir?'

'My samudi is Bana Bihari Tripathy. He is my younger daughter Madhuchhanda's father-in-law. Perhaps you know Madhuchhanda. Wasn't she your classmate? If you are going to Beheda you have to first cross a village named Firozpur—its name has been now changed to Srirampur. My samudi lives there. Bana Bihari Tripathy was a lawyer by profession. Do you know him? You may not. He told me that your reporter instigated the Doms of the village to throw a cow's bone into the Mahadev temple. That was the real reason behind the fight.'

'Whatever I know about Lalatendu, Sir....'

'Santoshbabu, you are a very simple man. You live in Bhawanipatna. He lives in Beheda, some seventy to eighty kilometres away from you. I doubt whether you get to meet him even once a month. My samudi's house is just two kilometres away from Beheda. He has watched Laltu grow up. Will he lie? Do you know that Lalatendu has prohibited the UP School of his village to celebrate Ganesh and Saraswati pujas for the last two years? Do you have any information on this?'

'Prohibited the pujas! But why?'

'That is the point. There lies the root. My samudi told me that the boy was getting funds from Christian institutes of foreign countries and encouraging the Adivasis and Harijans to become Christians!'

'If that is so, let me ask him. He is coming to meet me today.'

'If you ask him, will he tell you the truth? Don't you know that the Doms are cheats? Is it for no reason that they say that if the Dom cheats, you are ruined; if an egg cracks, it is spoilt!'

The doorbell rang. Mitali opened the door and said, 'He is at home. Come in.'

Lalatendu entered. His face was pale. His eyes showed that he had not slept all night.

'Ok then, Sir. Someone has come to visit me. I'll call you back. Bye, Sir.' Santosh Panda replaced the receiver of the phone and signalled to Lalatendu to take the chair facing him.

'I hear that a case has been filed against you?' asked Santosh.

'Dada, I had no idea about the case till yesterday,' said Lalatendu in a low voice. 'When I heard I went to enquire about it from the thana in-charge, Deepbabu, last night at ten o'clock. The villagers, it seems, in their FIR have written that I instigated the people of the Dompada to throw a cow's bone into the Mahadev temple.'

'But you told me that you were not there during the fight. Then how come the villagers mentioned your name...?'

'I don't know. Everyone knows that I was not there. After the fight I got the news and reached there. I really don't know what my fault is. And the story about the cow's bone has been cooked up; it is a complete lie, Dada.'

'And Lalatendu, I heard that since two years your village school has stopped celebrating Ganesh and Saraswati pujas?'

'Dada, you know that in schools and colleges students are from different castes and religions. Is it appropriate to celebrate any event of a particular religious group in educational institutes? Dada, our schools and colleges are forums for intellectual debates and discussions. Is it right to allow blind beliefs there? So we, the villagers, together took a decision to stop celebrating any religious occasion.'

'Are you saying that worshipping Ganesh and Saraswati is just a blind belief?'

'Dada, all gods and goddesses and the rituals relating to them are blind beliefs. If someone does not study but worship either Ganesh or Saraswati will they thrust knowledge into his or her brain?'

'But shouldn't the children get opportunities to learn our culture and tradition?'

'Who is stopping them from learning our culture and tradition? But, Dada, that does not mean that a custom of a particular group has to be forced upon all others. That is injustice.'

'What do you mean?'

'Suppose we take the example of Brajmohan High School here in Bhawanipatna. In it there are children from the Hindu, Christian, Muslim, and Sikh communities. Are the cultures and traditions of all these children one and the same? Every year the school celebrates only Ganesh and Saraswati pujas. But there are no celebrations during Easter or Id-ul-Fitr. Dada, by doing so are we not forcing the gods and goddesses of one community on the children of other communities?'

'Are there Christian children also studying in your village school?'

'Christians in our village? We have only four communities, the Gond, the Mali, the Gaud, and the Dom. And people of these communities are not Hindus. Dada, is it therefore right to force the Hindu gods and goddesses on them?'

'Have you gone mad or what? If you are not a Hindu then what are you?'

'Dada, if we were Hindus would there be prohibitions against Dom entry into temples? If we were Hindus would people who touch us be polluted? Don't we know who we are? We have a different culture and a tradition. Our culture is entirely different from yours. We are not Hindus.'

'Lalatendu, you raised the issue of untouchability. People of your community were considered untouchables because earlier they were eating beef....'

'Didn't I say our culture is different? For the Hindus the cow is the holy mother ... but her meat is food for us like your goat meat. And, Dada, I read in a book that in the past the Brahmins also ate beef.'

'Nonsense! It must have been propagated by either the Pathans or the Christians.'

'Not really, Dada. This is mentioned in the shastras and *samhitas* written by the Brahmins. It is only after Buddha spread the message of non-violence and kindness that the Brahmins stopped eating beef.'

'Do you have that book? Next time you come bring it. I would like to go through it.'

During this discussion Santosh Panda was shaken by doubts. In fact they were not mere doubts. He was almost convinced that Lalatendu was hiding several things from him. Perhaps everything Pumu told him was true. Is smoke without fire possible? Is Lalatendu then spreading anti-Hindu propaganda? Is he encouraging people to become Christians? Otherwise why did he argue so much against celebrating pujas in the school?

Santosh Panda did not want any further arguments with Lalatendu. In spite of being a Brahmin he knew nothing about the shastras or puranas other than stories from the Ramayana and the Mahabharata. He, of course, knew that Brahmins being born from Brahma's mouth were superior in caste hierarchy. Everybody else—Gonds, Gaudas, Malis, Telis, Kondhs, Bhatras, Doms, and Ghasis—were Sudras. They were all born from Brahma's feet and, therefore, low in caste hierarchy. They were the servants of the upper castes and it was their duty to serve.

But then, there were hardly any caste practices now. Where are the Brahmins who chanted the Gayatri Mantra both morning and evening? Instead of praying they were setting up hotels and shoe shops. Meanwhile the Doms and the Ghasis had become educated and were employed in various sectors. But that did not mean that Lalatendu could spread the rumour that Brahmins in ancient times ate beef! We do not hate you as a Dom. We drink tea together. Then why should you spread such elaborate lies against us? Pumu was right in saying that the Doms were cheats! So don't believe them! They use the same plate to both eat and shit.

'And, what shall we do with your case?' Santosh Panda asked to change the topic of the discussion.

'That's what I wanted to ask you. I'm not guilty. I think, behind all these conspiracies, Semi Agrawal has a role. Perhaps the news that we had published against his rice mill ... for that....'

'Whoever is behind this case we'll deal with him later. But now that a case has been registered against you....' Santosh Panda looked worried.

'If you explain everything in detail to the SP just once....' Lalatendu looked perplexed when he made this request.

'Will that old rat be caught easily? Ok, let's see, I'll request him. You also request the thana in-charge Deepbabu. He is from your community; he might listen to you.' After thinking for a while Santosh Panda asked, 'Have you written the news?'

Lalatendu pulled out a sheet of folded paper from his pocket and handed it over to him.

Glancing at the paper Santosh said, 'It's fine; I'll read it later. Now I've got some urgent work. When will you come again?'

After two days, a news item on the front page of the *Hastakshep* read:

A communal riot broke out after the bone of a cow was thrown into the Mahadev temple at Srirampur; fifteen people arrested including a reporter.

◆

Glossary

Aai	Grandmother
aaram	Rest
agreshara	To advance or move forward
Aja	Grandfather
alekh	Indescribable
Alekha baba	Follower of Mahima Dharma, a puritanical religious cult based on non-dualism, denial of priesthood, caste system, and idolatry
anna	One-sixteenth part of a rupee; char anna is twenty-five paise
arisha	Traditional Odia cake made of rice powder and molasses
asta prahari nama yagyan	Religious celebration performed continuously while chanting the names of Lord Ram and Krishna
babu	Son; also a term of respect while addressing an official
Bada Thakura	Lord Jagannath of Puri, the most famous deity of Odisha
Badu	Father's elder brother
bahuchori	Outdoor village game, literally, abduction of the bride; while one group tries to abduct the bride, the other tries to protect her

Baitarani	River in Odisha
bana	Ghost
Basant Panchami	Fifth day of the bright half of the tenth lunar month of Magha (mid-January to mid-February), when Saraswati, the Goddess of Learning, is worshipped
basti	Slum
behera	Waiter
bel	Wood apple
bhadi	Platform of wood or bamboo
Bhagabata	Purana authored by Jagannath Dasa of six-teenth century in praise of Vishnu
bhai	Brother
Bhainro	Rural, tribal god; another name for Shiva
Bhima	Local god known for his anger and strength; perhaps a derivative of the second Pandava brother of the Mahabharata
bididhungia	Tobacco rolled up in a tendu leaf and smoked
boudhik barga	Scholarly discussion
bratakatha	Story depicting the significance and impor-tance of a particular religious observance
Budharaja	Local god known for his generosity
Chaitpuni	Full moon night of the lunar month of Chaitra (March to April)
Chaitra Ghant	Religious procession of a local deity amidst folk music during Chaitra
chakuli	Thin, round flat cake made of rice and black gram powder
chakunda	Roadside plant which grows during monsoon

Chandaluni	Wife of an outcaste in Balaram Das's *Lakshmi Purana*, dated seventeenth century; even though she is an untouchable, Goddess Lakshmi visits her house because of her piety
chudaghasa	Flattened rice mixed with sugar, coconut, and dry fruits
chulha	Large hearth
chutney	Kind of sauce
Dada	Elder brother
Dadi	Grandfather
Daksha	Salute practised in the Rashtriya Swayamsevak Sangh training centre
dal	Gravy of mashed lentils
dalabat	Crossroads of a village
dalia	Broken wheat
dalma	Mixed curry of pulses and vegetables
debata	God
dhanda	Non-poisonous water snake
dharma	Sacred duty, religion, righteousness
dhawnra	Indigenous tree used for making the handle of an axe
dhol	Traditional musical instrument; a drum
dhoti	Clothing worn by men wrapped around the waist and tucked inside
Diyal Jatra	Deepavali, the festival of lights
Dom	Scheduled-caste community of Odisha
durbar	Court
dwaja pranam	Salute made to the flag in the Rashtriya Swayamsevak Sangh training centres
gahera	Thorny tree

gana	Person from an untouchable community appointed (in the past) by the village as its messenger
gana bhogra	Land given freely to the village messenger for performing traditional duties
ganja	Cannabis sativa
gauda	Milkman
gauduni	Wife of a milkman
gauntia	Village head
Ghasi	Scheduled-caste community of Odisha whose traditional occupation is sweeping the village roads and streets
ghee	Clarified butter
gidha	Traditional instrument for measuring grains; three gidhas of grain make a kilogram
Gond	Scheduled-tribe community of Odisha
goru haat	Cattle market
gudi	Small temple or a mud hut where deities are worshipped
gur	Molasses
haat	Market
habildar	Head constable
halia	Domestic and agricultural bonded worker
haribol	Chanting the name Hari
homa	Oblation of clarified butter into ritualistic fire; same as gheeapoda
Jalkamni	Local goddess
kabaddi	Outdoor Indian game of speed and breath control
Kaki	Aunt
Kalisundari Gudi	Place where Kalisundari, a local goddess, is worshipped

kandul	Red gram generally cultivated in hilly areas
Kapat Pasha	Odia rendering of the game of dice from the Mahabharata, a musical poem composed by Bhima Dhibara in the seventeenth century
Karan	Community of scribes in Odisha
Kavi Surya	Designation given to Baladev Rath, a famous Odia poet of the late eighteenth and early nineteenth centuries for his extraordinary contribution to poetry
Keshab Koili	Long narrative poem written by Markanda Dasa, supposedly around the beginning of the fifteenth century, in which Yashoda laments Krishna's absence by addressing a cuckoo
khichiri	Rice, pulses, and vegetables cooked together
khiri	Rice pudding
kho-kho	Outdoor Indian game played by twelve persons in two teams who try to avoid being touched by members of the opposing team
Kuber	God of Wealth
kurta	Long shirt
kusum	Fruit-bearing tree; oil is extracted from its seeds
Lakshmi handi	Earthen pot into which village women deposit a fistful of rice every time they cook a meal as a security for a time of need
lathi	Stick or baton
lengeda	Lame
linga	Image of Lord Shiva in the shape of a phallus, symbolizing his creative power
lula	Handicapped or weak
Ma	Mother

mahajan	Wealthy man or moneylender
mahana	Weight of forty seers
mahima	Glory
Mahima Tungi	Place where mendicants of Mahima Dharma congregate to worship
mahua	Flower from a local tree called mahula, used to make jaggery and country liquor
mahuli	Liquor prepared from the mahul flower
mahuria	Traditional trumpet blower
Mali	Community that sells puffed rice in the village, who come under the Other Backward Class category in Odisha
Mamu	Uncle
mana	Traditional instrument for measuring grain; one mana equals to two kilograms
margasira manabasha	Fast observed on all Thursdays in the month of Margasira (November to December) in honour of Lakshmi, the Goddess of Wealth
matra	Stroke relating to vowels
mehendi	Henna
mita	Friend
nirakar	Formless
niranjan	Untained, sinless
nishan	Traditional musical instrument; a drum
Nuakhai	Festival feast of the new harvest celebrated in western part of Odisha
pada	Neighbourhood
paisa	Coinage; a hundredth part of a rupee
palasa	Tree known as the flame of the forest
panakia	Multiplication table
Pangnia Budha	Old man expert in black magic

panishala	Place at the backyard of the house where clean water is stored in earthen pots
Pausapunei	Full moon night in the ninth lunar month of Pausha (mid-December to mid-January)
payas	Sweet dish made of rice, milk, and sugar or molasses
pika	Countrymade cheroot
pothipurana	Book, or palm-leaf manuscript, with religious themes
prahara	Eighth part of twenty-four hours
prasad	Offerings of food or fruits made to a deity
Pual Uwansh	Ritual observed by the villagers on the first day of the new moon in the month of Shravan (July to August) where a chicken is sacrificed to the village deity to ward off all kinds of diseases
puja	Worship
pujari	Priest
pukka	Concrete
Purana	Literally, old story, Hindu religious literature comprising legends and myths with a strong theistic character
puri	Small, round crisp cake deep fied in oil or clarified butter
puruna musha	Old rat
raktarani	Blood-red-coloured flower
saala	Abuse referring to one's brother-in-law in a derogatory sense
samhita	Refers to the most ancient layer of text in the Vedas, consisting of mantras, hymns, prayers, litanies, and benedictions

samudi	Father-in-law of son or daughter
Sankranti	First day of the solar month
sarpanch	Head of the panchayat
sasan	Village donated by a king to Brahmins
savarna	Upper caste
savitri brata	Fast observed by (Hindu) married women on the fifteenth day of the dark half of the month of Jyestha (May to June) for the welfare of their husbands
seo bundi	Mix of sev and bundi, prepared from chick-pea powder and deep fried; while sev is salty, bundi is sweet
shakha	Training centre organized by the Rashtriya Swayamsevak Sangh
shathia pauti	Sixty kilograms of rice cooked every day in the Jagannath temple in Puri as prasad for devotees
shirakaleshi	State when the energy of a spirit enters and takes possession of a human being
sinderi	Variety of mango
sindoor	Vermilion
singhan	Mucus
Sitachori	Poetic rendering on the theme of Sita's abduction by Ravana in the Ramayana
sudasa brata	Fast observed by Hindu women on Thursday falling on the tenth day of the bright half of a lunar month in honour of Lakshmi
suddhi	Purification rite
tasni	Small plate
teli	Traditionally an oilman
Teli Samaj	Members belonging to the oil press community

tendu	Local tree, the leaves of which are used for wrapping bidis
Thakurani	Goddess
thali	Big circular plate
thanababu	Police inspector
Thutimaili	Local goddess
Tretaya Yuga	Second of the four yugas the Hindus believe in, in which Ram, an incarnation of Vishnu, is believed to have come down to the Earth to restore dharma; the other yugas are Satya, Dwapara, and Kali
trishul	Trident
Tungi Gudi/ Tungudi	Cottage where mendicants of Mahima Dharma gather to worship
yajna	Ritualistic sacrifice
Yama	Hindu God of Death

About the Author and the Translator

 **Akhila Naik** hails from the Kalahandi district of Odisha. He is a postgraduate in Odia literature and has been teaching undergraduate students for nearly a decade. He writes poetry, short stories, and essays in Odia and regularly publishes them in Odia magazines and journals. *Bheda* is his first novel. Presently, he is teaching Odia literature in Government College, Bhawanipatna, Kalahandi, Odisha.

 **Raj Kumar** is a professor in the Department of English, University of Delhi. His research areas include autobiographical studies, Dalit literature, Indian writing in English, Odia literature, and postcolonial studies. He has been a fellow at the Indian Institute of Advanced Study, Shimla, in 1999 and has published in journals such as *Social Action*, *Indian Literature*, *Social Scientist*, *Journal of the School of Language, Literature and Culture Studies*, and *Economic and Political Weekly*. His book *Dalit Personal Narratives: Reading Caste, Nation and Identity* was published in 2010. He has also translated literary texts from Indian languages, especially Odia into English.